THI
They...
of th...
Muh...

THE ASSASSIN
Eric Schofield, successful writer on the contemporary music scene, had another name and another occupation; he was also known as Pisces, one of the world's most expensive and deadliest killers-for-hire.

MOSSAD
The Israeli espionage agency had declared Pisces their number one target for extermination in retaliation for the murder of one of that nation's ambassadors.

MARSHA
The beautiful young black woman with whom Pisces falls in love, only to discover she is the granddaughter of one of the Angels and a possible threat to his life.

Did Elijah Muhammad die a natural death?
Is the Nation of Islam controlled by four old men?
Read on...

THE BLACK ANGELS

by STERLING HOBBS

HOLLOWAY HOUSE PUBLISHING COMPANY
LOS ANGELES, CALIFORNIA

Published by
HOLLOWAY HOUSE PUBLISHING COMPANY
8060 Melrose Avenue, Los Angeles, California 90046

International Standard Book Number 0-87067-399-8
Printed in the United States of America
Cover illustration by William Lawrence Thon

Dedication

This book is for Kathy...
The Secretary of my State of Mind

For each (such person)
There are (angels) in succession,
Before and behind him:
They guard him by command
Of Allah. Verily never
Will Allah change the condition
Of a people until they
Change it themselves.

> *The Holy Quran*
> *Sura 13, Ayat 11*

Muhammad is only a Messenger.
Surely, many Messengers passed
Away before him. So, if
He dies or is
Assassinated will you then
Turn back upon your heels?
And whoever turns back
Upon his heels will not do
The least harm to Allah.
And Allah will reward
The Grateful.

> *The Holy Quran*
> *Sura 3, Ayat 144*

Prologue

The silver Mustang II cruised slowly along Michigan Avenue. The driver eyed the colorfully dressed women with intensity. Some were standing against the display windows of empty, darkened stores. Others strolled between the corners of the block, reaching the curb and reversing their direction, walking purposefully against the midnight chill.

Each woman flashed her most alluring smile at the passing car. Reaching the corner, the car pulled over to the curb and stopped. The driver appraised the ladies of the night and found a woman of every nationality on exhibit.

A medium height, very light-complexioned black woman approached the Mustang. She wore high heels, a short red dress and a jacket that was pulled tightly over her huge breasts. A blond wig tilted awkwardly on her head and revealed a small black plait curled beneath it.

"You dating baby?" she sang to the driver as she peered

into the passenger side window. The man ignored her. He slowly pulled the car away from the curb and drove leisurely until he reached another corner where similarly attired women were stationed.

A short Puerto Rican woman waved at the driver. He surveyed the numerous women. A plump, very dark black woman bounced over to the car as the driver pulled to a stop. Reaching the passenger side, she opened her coat, permitting the driver a view of her meaty legs and hips. She squeezed one breast and managed to produce, despite the cold and vicious night wind, a facial expression she thought to be seductive. The driver leaned over and lowered the window.

"What'll it be, daddy? Ten for a blow job. Twenty to fuck. Five if you just want me to jerk you off."

The driver looked past her to a tall, brown-complexioned woman who was dressed in a beige pants suit and black leather coat.

"Send her over," the driver commanded.

"Who? Her?" The woman, disappointed, looked over her shoulder at the taller woman.

"Yes. The one in the leather coat," the man stated.

"Shit," she mumbled. "Melody, he wants you," she called.

The tall woman glided over. She leaned over for a look at the driver then paused momentarily as if to decide whether to risk getting into the car with him.

"Get in," he said, making the decision for her. She slid into the car, curled her long legs beneath her and turned toward the driver.

He could see that she was quite striking. She dressed conservatively and was lacking the cheap, worn out appearance that her colleagues wore so proudly.

"How tall are you?" asked the driver.

"Five feet ten inches. Why?"

8

When the man said nothing, she said: "Mister, it's thirty for sex. Five for the room and . . ."

"Where's your room?" the man asked.

"The Fairview."

He turned left and headed toward the old hotel. The sleepy front desk clerk barely even looked up from the magazine he was reading when he tossed her a key. They boarded a rickety elevator and rode to the third floor. At room 304 the girl inserted a key.

The girl entered the room ahead of the man. He closed the door and handed her two twenties. She removed her jacket, kicked off her shoes and slid out of her pants. She stood before him with her hands on her hips. Her legs were long and slender, but well-shaped. Her small, firm breasts could be seen through the sheer material of her blouse.

"Take them off for me," she whispered. She knew that some johns liked to remove women's underwear. She was dog tired but she knew a little effort went a long way toward bringing customers back for more. Unlike some hookers, she wasn't at all opposed to mixing a little pleasure with business. But, as she'd already had five "dates" that night, her own passions had long ago been extinguished. This was purely business.

It's a shame, she thought, that this one hadn't come her way earlier tonight when she was horny as hell. He sure was a pretty nigger. Almost six feet tall. Slim. What in the world was a fine nigger like this doing buying pussy? He should have girls waiting in line for him.

"No. Keep your clothes on. I don't want to screw you," the man stated calmly.

On no! A weird one! What's he want, a beating? A golden shower? It was always the pretty ones who wanted the weirdest treatment. "Mister, if you want something freaky it's gonna cost you. And if you're thinking about beatin *me,* you can forget it.''

She looked at her pocketbook resting on the hotel's bureau. She kept a straight razor there.

Try something, motherfucker, and I'll slice that pretty face into a thousand pieces. Her thoughts thundered inside her head.

''I want something very special. I'll pay well for it.''

''What's your thing, man?''

Although he was speaking in low, calm tones she could sense the urgency in his voice. But there was another ingredient along with the urgency. She could feel danger in his voice.

''I want you to do something at 7:45 this morning. I need you for a half hour, from 7:45 till 8:15. I'll pay you a thousand dollars.''

''Buddy, I ain't about to drive no stickup cars, and if you think...''

''I don't want you to do anything illegal,'' he interrupted. ''It's, well, it's like a little game I play. Put your clothes back on. I'll explain what I want.''

She made no move to re-dress. Being naked, she felt within her environment. Her nudity, she felt, gave her a certain kind of power.

He explained what he wanted her to do.

''I don't know if I understand,'' she said after a while. ''Just sit in the lobby for about twenty-five minutes and then run out?''

''Yes.''

''You're paying a grand for that? How do I know you're not up to something and you want me to attract the heat off you? I'm not stupid, you know.''

''No, it's nothing like that. I just have this fantasy. Oh, this is embarrassing. Maybe we should forget it.''

''No, go on. Explain.'' She was thinking about the money.

10

"See, uh, I always wanted to rape a nurse," the man said. His face was contorted with embarrassment.

"Oh," said the woman. "I think I understand. You want me to dress up like a nurse. Come running out of Mercy Douglas Hospital. And what? You're gonna grab me or something?"

The man looked downward in shame. "Yeah. That's it. But, look. If you don't want to . . ."

"Don't worry about it. Plenty of people act out their fantasies. You got some nurse clothes—a uniform—in my size?"

The man nodded. "The outfit is in the car."

She'd met plenty of weirdos before, but something told her that this one would take the cake. She knew some men got off on chasing women and faking like they were raping them. Gave them a feeling of power or something. What the fuck? For a thousand dollars she'd run the marathon.

Chapter One

April, 1974

He was in the center of the ring and Joe Frazier rushed toward him, smoking. He threw punches at Frazier's head. The punches were on target, but the head continued to bob and weave and advance closer. Frazier, so close now that he could smell his sweat, leaped off the floor and slammed a crushing left hook against his head. His knees buckled and his legs wobbled.

"If I go down," he thought, "everybody'll laugh at me and then I'll die."

He fell into the ropes and there was Joe, breathing hotly against his neck and face. He wanted to touch Frazier; wanted to tell him that he, of all the people in the world, understood him best.

But Joe banged punches against his ribs.

"If you don't fight I'll have to stop it," a voice shouted

angrily at him. He realized that it was the referee. But he couldn't see the ref. He couldn't see anyone, except a bruised, bleeding Joe Frazier who was slamming his body and his head with savage punches.

Feebly at first, then with rapid speed, he began to fight back. Both fighters were drenched with blood. He didn't know if the blood was Frazier's or his own. He wanted to taste it, to see if it was his. But he knew that if he stopped throwing punches, even for a moment, Joe Frazier would surely knock him out.

Initially, with some amusement, and then with a growing sense of horror, he realized that his punches were passing right through Frazier. But Smokin' Joe's punches were not passing harmlessly through him. They were connecting.

Flames, mixed with smoke now, streamed from Frazier's ears and nose. Joe lunged forward, smashing him with a classic left hook. He went down. Joe loomed over him, sweat and piss raining down on him from beneath Joe's blood-soaked trunks.

In the distance he heard bells ringing. Incessantly ringing. Someone screamed, "Saved by the bell!"

Under the power of instinct, Eric Schofield's hand crawled over to the nightstand where his telephone screamed at him furiously.

"What round is it?" he whispered sleepily into the phone.

"What?" a female voice answered back. "Eric, is that you?"

"Tracey?" He was becoming gradually reoriented to the real world.

"What in the world have you been drinking?" the woman asked over the phone.

"Tracey, hold on for just one minute."

He laid the phone down and sat on the edge of the bed. He shook his head violently from side to side. Then he rose and walked cautiously to the bathroom. He ran cold water and splashed his face with it liberally.

That was some dream!

His head was clearer now and he wanted a cigarette. He walked back into the room and, instead of Winstons, Tareytons were laying on his dresser.

Then he remembered the girl. They'd gotten drunk together. He'd run out of cigarettes and had to smoke her Tareytons. In drunken humor they joked about Tareyton smokers preferring to fight than switch. Somehow that led to a mock fight on top of the bed and a fall into each other's arms, making love.

That's where that crazy dream must have come from.

He lit a Tareyton and wrinkled his face in protest against the dry, empty taste. He picked up the phone.

"You still there?"

"Do you realize I've been waiting for five minutes?"

"You're exaggerating."

"What was all that stuff about rounds?"

"I was dreaming."

"You must've had a wild night. The phone rang twenty times."

"Exaggerating again," he said.

"How would you know if I was or not. You were dead to the world. Where's the dame you spent the night with?"

"She left. I guess."

"Here. Let me describe her for you. She was tall with big legs. And the thing that attracted her to you most was her fascinating anatomy. Her brain was located beneath her navel." The woman laughed into the phone.

"Yeah. That sounds about right," sighed Schofield.

"See? I know you like a book. You don't let your hair down that much, but when you do I bet you're explosive."

"Wanna find out?"

"No thank you, Casanova."

"Well," Eric said, "if you didn't call to excite my passions, then that one-track mind inside your lovely head must be concerned with business." He pronounced "business" as though it was a dirty word.

"Guess what?" she teased.

"You're pregnant."

"Come on. Guess what?"

"I'm guessing. You sound like a little kid. Just tell me, will you? I'm a terrible guesser."

"I sold your book to Dunn and Lowery," she said.

"No shit. Damn, that was fast."

"It's a good book. A very good book," she said.

"Aw, I bet you say that to all future Nobel laureates."

"And they're going to do a heavy promotion thing, Eric. Real heavy."

She paused for a moment. When he made no comment she said, "When can you come to New York?"

"What for?"

"Well, for one thing, I thought you might like to pick up your advance."

"How much is it for?"

"Fifty."

"Fifty? *Thousand?*" He was incredulous.

"Like I said, they have big plans for this book."

"I'll be there," said Eric Schofield, "on the next thing smoking."

Three hours later he was on the Metroliner from Philadelphia's 30th Street Station going to Pennsylvania Station in New York. Late that afternoon he arrived in New York. As soon as he climbed the steps from the platform to the main floor he heard a woman's voice calling his name.

He turned to see Tracey Bivens trotting in his direction. She cut deftly through pedestrian traffic, exploiting the maneuverability of her small frame. She stood 4'10'' and weighed all of ninety pounds. Watching her, Schofield smiled. He was thinking that she moved like a halfback through a broken field.

When she reached him, Eric scooped her up in his arms and spun her around, her tiny legs almost knocking the briefcase from a passing commuter's hands.

"Put me down, fool," she said.

"Not till you tell me that you love me and only me."

"Right now I hate you. Come on, Eric. I don't like this kind of horseplay."

"Horseplay? Here I am ready to confess my undying love and you call it horseplay." He folded her in his arms and carried her effortlessly to the newsstand in the middle of the station's main floor. She struggled to free herself from Schofield's clutches.

"Doesn't the *New York Post* have a good sports section?" he asked, dropping coins inside a metal dish and taking a paper while he held her with his other arm.

"Put me down," she said.

"But actually, the *Daily News—Philadelphia Daily News*—has an even better sports section."

"Eric, this is no longer even remotely funny. Will you *please* put me down?"

"Now we got a guy named Stan Hochman. Helluva sports writer. Better than your Maury Allen if you ask me."

"Eric! I'm going to scream!"

"Do you love me yet? Or do you still hate me?"

"Yes! Now please put me down."

"You know, you sound like a broken record."

He placed her gently onto the floor. Some passersby smiled in amusement at the two of them, thinking them lovers. Others, conforming more to the personality of New York, afforded them no more than a casual glance.

Tracey, one hand on her hip and the other pointing at Eric, said: "If you ever pull a stunt like that I'll. . .I'll. . .kill you!"

"Oh please don't kill me, Tracey," he said in mock terror. He began to laugh and moments later the sound of Tracey's own laughter merged with his.

"Schofield, you need help," she said. "You are generously insane."

Tracey Bivens had spent three years establishing herself as a competent, no-nonsense literary agent. The kind of incident that had just occurred was hardly in accord with the image she'd cultivated.

Schofield knew how hard she worked to appear the quintessence of sophisticated black womanhood. And to him, her efforts were comical. He liked Tracey a lot. He counted her among his best friends. Of course, he'd flirted with her numerous times, but she would never hesitate to let him know that there was nothing happening. So she was just a very good friend, and he liked her so much he really didn't mind that he'd never succeeded in getting her into his bedroom.

More than his agent, Tracey was his teammate. He saw his book as a joint effort. And Tracey went far beyond the duties of an agent in getting Schofield's work published. Often she was his editor, advisor, cheerleader, and—when he'd permit it—his publicist.

Tracey had sold Eric's first book, a biography of Sam Cook entitled *The Cooker*. It was also the first book she'd ever sold as a literary agent. She'd gotten him a $5,000 advance and the book sold modestly.

His next book, *Sweet Soul Music,* did much better. It became the definitive work on black popular music. Eric traced the history of soul music from the '50s to 1970. He focused not just upon the big named stars, but also on the little known but immensely significant contributors to the soul sound: the arrangers, the producers, the composers, the lyricists, the studio session musicians and even the background singers.

Within the industry, certain drummers and bassists are legendary. But their names, before the publication of *Sweet Soul Music,* were virtually unknown beyond the walls of the studio.

Schofield, of course, also dealt with the singers themselves. He gave a profile and short biography of the musical giants, like Aretha Franklin, and the lesser known but immensely talented artists like Linda Jones whose one hit, "Hypnotized," was a haunting love song which continued to articulate lovers' painfully sweet emotions long after Linda's own premature death.

Sweet Soul Music, perhaps intentionally, made waves in the music industry. In a chapter called, "First I look At The Purse," capitalizing on a single of the same name by the Contours, Eric showed that very few blacks were getting rich off soul music. And most black singers, he predicted, would retire broke.

To Schofield, Marvin Gaye's *What's Going On* album was the crowning achievement of the last two decades of soul music. He even called it the best musical achievement in twenty years for any classification of music.

Critics, thinking that was a bit much, leaped all over him for that remark. What about the Beatles? What about Sinatra? What of Jimi Hendrix, John Coltrane, Bob Dylan and Miles Davis?

But Schofield stuck by his guns. He called *What's Going On* "an album born of desperation." It was an album Marvin had to write for his own survival and for his own self-respect as an artist. Schofield wrote: "Intense disgust with world socio-economic inequality, personal loneliness, sadness, near-despair along with keen social perspicacity and in

18

infinite depth of genius—and perhaps more than a little madness—were the ingredients that went into Gaye's haunting cry to a dying planet.''

Sweet Soul Music took off like a NASA space shot and established Eric Schofield as a leading authority on black music. Colleges across the country found the book extremely useful as an auxiliary text in music courses.

Schofield's approach to the singers and their music was analytical, hard-hitting and compassionate, but never sycophantic. When interviewing, he asked very tough questions, but not in an abusive manner. And if he thought a star was feeding him a line of bullshit, he didn't hesitate to say so.

Schofield's writing reflected sensitivity and empathy with artists which, being rare among writers who covered their acts, made him very popular among black entertainers. Where once he had to literally stop an elevator between floors to obtain an interview with a female superstar, now his name alone was sufficient to get singers to make room for him in their schedules.

Schofield, however, was not as admired by the disc jockeys and program directors of the nation's soul radio stations. He criticized the programming for only playing a minute percentage of the hundreds of records released yearly, and even then they selected the most juvenile ones for airplay. He accused the stations of spinning records at random with no attempt to set or create a mood. He characterized the jocks as crude, shallow, unsuccessful street hustlers who stroked their own egos over the air to compensate for their lack of real life success.

He criticized the program directors for insisting that the jocks limit their selection of records for airplay to only those current hits that were hot on the charts. Yet there was a wealth of oldies which listeners still desired to hear and which would serve to round out the overall program. The failure of radio stations to widen the range of their music choices prompted Schofield to raise questions of payola.

Besides, he reminded, most "soul stations" were white owned.

Eric and Tracey were shown to their tables at Sweet's restaurant in lower Manhattan. Eric ordered their wines, pronouncing the French names accurately. Impressed with his accent, the waiter asked, in French, if Eric spoke the language. When Eric replied that he did, the very prim waiter smiled broadly and spoke for a few moments with Schofield in his native tongue. Tracey failed to understand a word they were saying.

"I didn't know you spoke French."

"Had it for a few years in school. Polished it up later."

"In the Army?" she asked.

"Yeah."

"It's hard for me to imagine you as a soldier. Yet I know you did two tours in Vietnam. Do you speak any other languages?"

"Vietnamese, Chinese, German and Arabic," he said.

"Wow! I had no idea. What made you decide to learn so many languages?"

"Uh, in the Army I . . ." He stopped abruptly. "Hey, let's order lobster."

During the meal Tracey mused over how Eric, whenever his Army life was mentioned, found a way, no matter how awkward, to change the subject.

They ate in silence. Tracey thought of Eric's sudden shifts in mood. Though he'd said nothing to indicate it, she was sure that he had descended into one of his melancholy moods.

"You want to talk about the book?" she ventured. Her voice was utilizing its most soothing tone. She'd learned to treat her writer gently when he dipped into one of his silent bags. Sometimes she wondered if the guy was schizo or something.

"You think I'm crazy, don't you?" His question sounded almost like a plea, but it startled Tracey. She realized that she'd been looking at him in a peculiar manner.

"What makes you ask a thing like that?" she asked, aware of the fact that she'd responded too quickly.

Schofield had an unnerving habit of seemingly picking up on people's thoughts. After a while he said, "Tracey, I don't wanna do no promotions. You know I can't stand that shit." His face tightened. He seemed like he was in pain.

"Eric, I know you dislike doing television interviews and all that, but Dunn and Lowery have budgeted a lot of money for your book. And you know advertisements don't always sell books. Books are more personal. Potential buyers want to see *you*. Besides, ads are too expensive. This is your first novel, so it's like we have to start all over again. *Lovetown* can be a real big one, but only if you help push it. You know the circuit. The Merv Griffin Show, Mike Douglass, Carson if we can swing it, try to get somebody from *Playboy* to interview you, Phil Donahue, the whole works. That's what it'll take. The company is willing to push, but it won't do any good if you're gonna kill the thing before it's even started. We can make the *Times'* bestseller list with a whole lot of hustle and a little luck."

Schofield peered into his glass. After several seconds he said, "I really appreciate what you're doing, but I just can't do it. I can't go on TV. You . . . there are things you just don't understand."

"Understand what!" she snapped. "That you're too scared to give your own book a chance? No, I *don't* understand. I don't understand *you*. You write a great novel, one that could go all the way, and you won't help it sell. Writers are

21

dying for the kind of promo I've arranged for you. Why do you even bother to write at all, Eric Schofield? Kindly tell me that!''

Sheepishly, Schofield said, ''I didn't do anything on the last book. And it sold pretty well.''

''Pretty well!'' She was nearly shouting. ''Pretty fuckin' well! That book could've been a monster! You hear me? A monster! But you wouldn't go on TV so we had to move it at a snail's pace. We were damned lucky, that's all. But if you would have helped out just a little, we might've sold millions!''

She stopped as if to catch her breath, then continued.

''No, I'm sick of it! I had to twist arms and work for weeks to get the kind of deal I got you. Not just the advance, but the promotion budget. And do you care? 'I can't do it,''' she mimicked. ''Fuck it! You get yourself another agent. I've had it with you and your selfish bullshit!''

She rose from her seat and stormed out of the restaurant onto the now darkened streets of Manhattan.

Schofield wasn't sure how long he'd been walking, but he thought it had been for at least a couple of hours. Usually he hated the crowded, rushing streets of Gotham, which was why he refused to move from his apartment in Sharon Hill, Pennsylvania, despite the fact that much of his work took him to New York. Not only were his agent and publisher based in the City, but most of the entertainers he interviewed either lived in New York or visited there frequently. But Sharon Hill—about ten miles from Philadelphia—was as close to the Big Apple as he ever intended to live.

At this moment, however, he was grateful for the round-the-clock hoards who crammed New York's streets. He achieved a sort of anonymity in the midst of the throng. And that was the backdrop he required to sort out his scrambled thoughts.

22

This thing he had with writing had gone way too far. What was once a side interest, a hobby (despite Laura's insistence upon calling it a "career") had mushroomed into something that was becoming increasingly problematic.

The writing itself—and even the time consuming research—posed no real problems because he was a fast writer and he found research educationally stimulating and therefore easy.

But now he had, unintentionally and unexpectedly, stumbled upon the threshold of national fame. One trip around the talk-show circuit and he could forget about his cherished anonymity. Publicity was the last thing he desired. It was one of the few things he could not afford.

Tracey was mad at him. Madder than he'd ever seen her before. Well, so what? Maybe it was best to forget about the damn book. Things had gotten quite out of hand. If Tracey couldn't respect his wishes, too bad. He was sorry that she'd wasted her energy and time, but that's how it was. She had no right to leap all over him in that restaurant. Sure, they were close, but not that close.

It was beginning to drizzle slightly. A man stepped out of a record shop in front of Eric. "Excuse me, sir. You got the time?" Eric asked.

"Quarter after ten, Mac."

The drizzle picked up, becoming a moderate rainfall. Eric strolled on, oblivious to it.

For some reason, the hurt he'd seen in Tracey's eyes was messing with his mind—or heart. She did hustle, he had to give her credit for that. Eric recalled how she'd told him that she'd wanted to be a writer in the worst way.

"But my words were sterile. They had no magic," she had said. "Oh, the grammar was perfect and my writing was coherent, but it was *dead,* if you know what I mean."

She'd taken a job with a public relations firm, but she

longed for a place in the literary world. Then, a guy she was dating, Nathan Spring, informed her of an opening at Snoden and Associated Literary Agency. Acting on impulse (she knew next to nothing about representing writers) she applied and, to her own surprise, got the job.

After going three months without a single sale she was ready to hang it up and become a school teacher or something. When you grow up, she told herself, you have to be realistic. Since her mother and two of her sisters were school teachers, her idea of realism was teaching school, an idea she loathed.

Hopping over a puddle on the sidewalk, Eric wondered what Tracey was doing at that very moment. Despite her temper, she was really a sweet girl. They were just friends— or at least they were friends before the last blowup—but if it weren't for his work, his *real* work, who knows? Sure, Tracey had turned him down every time he hit on her. But he was sure that if he ever was truly serious, she'd give in. But that was, perhaps, just his male egotism sounding off. Just wishful thinking on his part.

He wondered if television exposure would truly endanger him that much. Most of the times when he carried out a contract he was in disguise. And on the few occasions that he wasn't, the only possible witness was a person who would speak no more, at least not in this world.

Yet there was always the off chance that someone looking out of a window, or standing unseen in the shadows, had seen his face. And seeing him on television might trigger their memory.

But what were the chances of that occurring? A hundred to one? A million to one? Maybe he was being *too* careful.

A taxi turned the corner. Schofield hailed it.

"Lenox Terrace," he told the driver after he settled into the backseat.

"Sorry, Bub. I don't go to Harlem."

Schofield thought of the decals he'd seen on several gypsy cabs in New York: "We're not yellow. We go anywhere." This cab and its pilot were both yellow.

Without speaking Eric pushed a ten dollar bill through the tray in the glass partition. The driver took it.

"On second thought," he said, "I should get to see more of the city now and then."

Chapter Two

Tracy Bivens stepped out of the shower. She wrapped herself in a large towel and stepped from the small bathroom into her bedroom.

She finished drying off and applied lotion to her small, shapely body. She walked in front of a mirror and looked at her image. The slight sag to her small breasts was nearly imperceptible. She felt she'd gained maybe two pounds over the winter, but now that warm weather had come she was sure to burn them off soon. But, she thought vainly, the extra weight didn't really look too bad. All two pounds of it seemed to have accumulated on her posterior.

Her eyes traveled down to her small legs. She'd always been self-conscious about her legs, thinking them too thin. So she wore pants to cover them. Then a boyfriend she had, a self proclaimed "leg man," told her: "Your legs aren't okay, they're beautiful. It ain't the size that makes legs look good; the shape and skin texture are more important than slabs of meat.''

Now she liked her legs. She still wished they were bigger, but they were well-shaped. But she remained self-conscious about her feet. Size sevens, average for most women, she thought were far too big for a woman of her height.

Just a couple of weeks ago Eric had told her that her feet were sexy. Now just what was sexy about feet?

"No, I'm serious," he had insisted. "Never met a girl yet with big feet who couldn't get down between the sheets. You should model shoes.''

She laughed to herself thinking of nutty Eric. But her smile died when those thoughts took her back to the events of the evening. That damned Eric. Selfish bastard didn't give two damns about how she worked her butt off for him and his damn book.

She admitted to herself that in all likelihood she could make the deal stick even without Eric's participation in promotional activities. But she was also concerned about him as a person and as a writer. He had so much potential. He was a natural. Eventually, he might become another James Baldwin. Maybe even another Norman Mailer. Well, she could dream if she wanted to, couldn't she?

She wondered why she was taking this so personally. She knew how difficult Eric could be. She had already made up her mind that she was going to keep her cool and patiently nudge him into agreeing to do at least a little promotional work. She knew, beforehand, that he was going to resist. But she also knew that she could bring him around, eventually.

Then he had to go into one of his stupid quiet moods. She'd just gotten him a super contract and there he was sitting there looking sullen. They should have been celebrating, not brooding.

27

Right in her purse was a bank draft for fifty thousand dollars. Her company would get 10% and Eric would get the rest. Now she would have to mail it to him. She'd split so fast that she hadn't had the chance to even show him the check. That was what made her blow her cool, she thought. His lack of appreciation.

She searched her bureau for her sexiest nightie. She also found a joint she'd rolled up days ago. She seldom smoked herb, but her nerves were on edge, and she could use a little calming.

She padded barefoot into the living room. Another huge mirror greeted her there. She scrutinized her reflection again and decided that, in that negligee, she could cause a monk's nature to rise.

She selected an album by Harold Melvin and the Bluenotes from her collection. She put the record on, settled herself comfortably upon the sofa, and fired up the joint.

The voice of the Bluenotes' lead singer, Theodore Pendergrass, entered her ears. For some reason she associated the words of the song that was playing, "If You Don't Know Me By Now," with Eric Schofield. She and Eric knew each other far too well to be going through arguments like they'd had tonight. Still, she was furious with him. If we were married I'd divorce the bum.

Her own thoughts surprised her. She'd never thought of him in such terms before. So where'd that deviate thought come from? Of course, she'd long been attracted to him in a certain kind of way. But she'd made up her mind long ago that there could never be anything romantic between them. First of all, business and romance didn't make for a good mixture. Secondly, Eric never seemed to take women seriously. They were a mere diversion. She could never see him putting a woman first in his life. Something else consumed his time and attention. And it wasn't writing. He didn't put all that much of himself into his work. Just enough to write great stuff. But she knew he could do even more, if he cared enough.

Whatever it was, it was enough to keep her from allowing Eric's come-ons to ever get anywhere. He was the kind of dude that a girl could wake up and find herself hopelessly in love with. And his heart would be somewhere else. Not necessarily with another woman. Just somewhere else.

And thirdly, there was her career. That same career that'd stopped her from marrying Nathan Spring, a man she'd loved. But she was driven to make her own mark. But Nathan wanted her to be a lawyer's wife, to give up her own work and costar in the theater of his life. No go. He packed up, threw their relationship to the wind, and pushed off to Washington, D.C.

Drawing on the last part of the joint she reflected on her first encounter with Eric Schofield.

The nut had sent an unsolicited manuscript to Snoden and Associates. It was company policy to return, unread, all unsolicited manuscripts. One of the secretaries was about to send Eric's stuff back to him, but Eric had enclosed a photograph of himself. He was so attractive that the secretary decided to pass the photo around to the other girls in the office.

When it reached Tracey's desk she had asked, "Who's this handsome player?"

"Another would-be writer," she was told, "who sent us an unsolicited manuscript which we're going to return unread."

Tracy was far from busy. She had yet to make her first sale and had pretty much made up her mind to call it quits. Breaking company policy, she asked to see the manuscript and decided to read it until she got bored.

The cover page read: "The Cooker: The Life and Music

of Sam Cook.''

Like most young blacks, Tracey knew a lot about Sam Cook's music, but very little about his life. She was still very young when Sam was big.

She took the manuscript home with her and began to read. She read thirty pages and didn't get bored. Instead, she was fascinated.

Schofield's account of Cook's life was so moving, so touching, that it put you right there. She read the entire manuscript and, when she got to the part describing Cook's death, partially nude in a motel, she cried.

The next day she told her boss that she'd found a manuscript that she wanted very much to represent. He was reluctant, but decided to let her have a try.

When she dialed Schofield's number, he answered the phone: ''Rockefeller residence. David speaking.''

Tracey laughed. ''Mr. Rockefeller,'' she had said, ''that was one helluva book you wrote.''

''Who's this?'' He was startled. Obviously he'd been expecting someone else.

After meeting Schofield though, Tracey learned that as cheerful as he could be one moment, he could be sullen and moody the next. He was one complex dude.

The Cooker was the first book she sold. She broke into tears of happiness when the publisher called informing her that they were going to publish the book.

Eric, she reflected, had seemed more happy for her success than for his own. He'd sent her flowers and a card, a card she kept still, that said: ''Selling your first book is like having your first baby. Congratulations.''

He was such a nut. And yet, that was exactly how she felt. She'd never had a child but, instinctively, she knew how it would feel: relief and a wonderful tiredness from delivery. Feeling empty and full at the same time. And a strange sorrow, as though something had been lost forever. That special, exclusive possession, that oneness with the child, would be lost forever. Now it would have to be shared with the world. They would never be quite as close—mother and child/agent and book—as they had been.

It was silly, but that was how she felt. Eric's book had been her baby, her exclusive possession. And she alone had recognized its value. Yes, he had indeed captured her emotional state of that moment. He had understood.

That was precisely the talent she lacked; the ability to instantly comprehend a complex emotional situation and translate it into simplified words which managed to retain the energy and the essence of what was being felt and experienced. That's what made the writer.

A new album had fallen onto the turntable, "I'll Always Love My Momma" by the Intruders. She heard a cut called "I Wanna Know Your Name."

Her boyfriend, Nathan, and she had broken up over a year ago. But tonight she wished he was there. Reefer always had an aphrodisiac effect on her. In fact, she realized, she'd only had sex a few times since she and her man had called it quits. And those experiences had been most disappointing. Out of curiosity more than anything else, she had bought a vibrator. But as the song says, "Ain't nothing like the real thing, baby."

Yet, oddly enough, it wasn't Nathan's face that came to her mind during these moments when her loneliness was giving way to more erotic feelings. She realized that it wasn't Nathan she longed for at all. It was, of all people, that nutty, complicated, conceited, selfish, good looking s.o.b. Eric Schofield! Damn! She was ashamed of herself. Longing for Eric was almost incestuous. Plus, feelings like those would bring nothing but trouble.

Having heard enough of the Intruders, she put on Marvin

Gaye's "Let's Get It On." Instead of the album, she chose the eight track tape. She wanted it to play again and again.

Tracey bounced to the beat of "Come Get to This" and jumped, startled, when the doorbell rang. Where was the doorman? People weren't supposed to just walk upstairs without her being notified first.

She walked to the door. It was securely locked as all Harlem apartments must be.

"Who's there?" she asked.

The voice sounded far away and frightened. Almost like a small boy afraid of rejection.

"It's Eric," said the voice.

She popped the locks and flung open the door.

"Come on in, you idiot," she said grinning.

He stood there, eyes suddenly wide. Then she remembered the negligee.

"You coming in or must I come out?"

Eric came in.

"I...uh...I was thinking..."

"Look at you," she said. "You're soaking wet."

"Oh, I'm sorry. I'm dripping water all over your rug."

"Screw the rug. What happened?"

"I was walking, thinking about, well, about you. I guess it started raining."

"You're a crazy kid, you know that? Thirty years old and still a crazy kid. Come on. You gotta get out of those wet things before you catch pneumonia."

She helped Eric remove his drenched garments.

"And take off these socks too," she admonished.

Stripped to his briefs, Eric looked up embarrassed. "These too?" he asked.

"Those too."

While Eric pulled off his underwear she went into the bathroom and returned with a towel.

"I feel kinda stupid," Eric said.

"Shut up," she replied.

She dried his head, his chest and back, his upper thighs and then his groin. At her touch his phallus began to grow.

Another cut off the Marvin Gaye tape was playing on the stereo.

Oh baby, please turn yourself around. Oh baby so I can love you good. I'll make you feel so good, awww sugar, just like you want me to . . . Oh baby, you sure love to ball. Oh honey, honey, you sure love to ball.

She returned to finish drying him off. Then she dropped the towel and gently stroked his penis. Then, raised on her tip toes, she pressed herself against him. Breathing hard, he kissed her neck. She undid a button and her nightie fell away.

Marvin Gaye crooned on in the background.

Chapter Three

The Israeli Prime Minister pounded the table furiously. In his rage, his conversation shifted from Yiddish to Hebrew to German to English. Presently, he was speaking in English.

"I want to know what in the hell is going on. A whole month has passed and what do you bring me? Nothing! Goddamnit! You are supposed to be in possession of the foremost intelligence network in the world and you can't give me any information? Cowshit!"

The director of MOSSAD was tempted to inform his lifelong friend, the Prime Minister, that the correct American expression was "bullshit," not cowshit. But this hardly seemed the time.

"Mr. Prime Minister," he began formally, "while it's true that we haven't apprehended the ambassador's assassin yet, we have made considerably more progress than a number of other agencies could have made under similar circumstances.''

The Prime Minister glared at the director. He wouldn't give him the satisfaction of hearing him ask what paltry information they'd scraped up.

"What we've learned," the director continued, "is that the Palestinians had nothing to do with Ambassador Yacob's murder."

The Prime Minister almost leaped from his chair. His face was blood red. His eyes bulged from his large head.

"What are you saying? What kind of mad scenario have you idiots dreamed up this time?"

"It's no scenario, Mr. Prime Minister. And I think you know," said the director, annoyed, "that our findings can hardly be deemed mad or idiotic. When we produce a theory, we are very rarely far from the mark."

The director paused. He knew the Prime Minister was only letting off steam but, hell, he'd been awake for almost three days, personally digging for the information he'd accumulated and he didn't enjoy being the Prime Minister's personal whipping boy when he was dead on his feet from overwork.

The day after the ambassador was murdered, Israeli jets, on the Prime Minister's orders, struck deep inside Lebanon killing scores of people. The planes' targets were PLO bases, but it turned out that more civilians were hit in the raids than actual PLO soldiers. Palestinian guerrillas were hidden so deeply within the mass of civilian Palestinians that it was almost impossible to strike guerrillas without killing civilians in the process.

Courtesy calls were made to leaders in the Knesset (the Israeli parliament) only after the strike had occurred. No one had been consulted prior to the raid.

The Palestinians, predictably, screamed outrage at the loss of civilian lives. The Israeli government had been criticized more than it was accustomed to in the Western press.

If it turned out that the Palestine Liberation Army had no connection with the ambassador's murder, there would surely be an international outcry. And the government of Prime Minister Uri Moshe could very possibly face a no confidence vote.

"So, if it wasn't the Palestinians, who was it?" the Prime Minister questioned.

"Americans."

"What is this, Benjamin? Some kind of ugly joke?"

"Uri, sit down," the director said softly.

The Prime Minister sat down, but stared at the director of MOSSAD in simmering rage. Benjamin Shiva was one of Moshe's most trusted friends. But Shiva had a habit of not telling the Prime Minister what was going on in his own country unless he absolutely had to. From anyone else, this would be intolerable. Even from his lifelong companion it was irksome.

"Uri, there are things that you don't completely understand. The Americans are frightened. Very frightened. Another war, they believe, would totally cut off their oil from the Persian Gulf and the rest of the OPEC states. This, so soon after the last embargo, they cannot afford. They believe that such an embargo would force them to take military action to seize the oil fields. Of course, such an act would provide the Soviets with an excuse for a direct confrontation. In all probability, this would lead to nuclear war. Of this the Americans are very afraid."

"Well what does any of this have to do with Yacob? We weren't prepared for war. What's all this mean to us?" The Prime Minister removed his glasses and, not finding tissue, wiped them with his necktie.

"The ambassador was in New York. He had visited a number of banks and other financial institutions. He was

36

exploring the possibility of securing extensive loans in the event another war should break out and our defense costs should spiral. Evidently, the Americans got wind of the ambassador's activities and panicked, thinking we were much closer to war than we, in fact, were.''

"This is crazy! I get the Foreign Ministry reports daily. Not once was Ambassador Yacob even mentioned in connection with such a mission."

"He wasn't sent by the Foreign Ministry," said Shiva.

"What? Who else has the authority to..."

"MOSSAD. He was MOSSAD," said the director dryly.

"Jesus Christ!" Whenever the Prime Minister used English he slipped into American expressions. "I never knew..." he stopped. "Who else do you have on my staff?" It was more an accusation than a question.

"That is not information that is available. Not even to you. You may fire me, Uri, and still I will not tell you. Nor will my successor. You know the rules."

"Jesus H. Christ!" exclaimed the Prime Minister.

"Of course," the director continued, "we cannot allow this information to get out."

"If I understand you correctly, you're telling me that the Americans knew of this secret mission you'd sent Yacob on, and that with him gone we'd be set back for quite a while, perhaps months, trying to arrange the financing. Am I correct?"

"Yes. So they made it look like a PLO hit so that we'd strike, but we'd be far from a full scale war."

"Who made the actual hit?" asked the Prime Minister. "Was it CIA? Did they hire somebody from the outside? An Arab?"

"We're not sure. Not yet. He could be an Arab, but then again he might be any nationality."

"Do you know anything at all about him?" asked the Prime

Minister.

"We think they hired a professional assassin. We don't think they used one of their own. Too risky. We are of the opinion that they went free lance on this one. Also, bear in mind that certain members of the American financial community function as governments within governments. It is not inconceivable that one of these sub-governments, not the U.S. government per se, was responsible for the hit." He yawned involuntarily. He was truly tired. "At any rate, we do have a partial identity of our man."

"Then come out with it!" The Prime Minister had lost all patience. "Who is it?"

"The man we seek has been used by organized crime in America, by the Japanese communists, by the IRA, maybe even by M16. They say he was involved with the assassination of Amilcar Cabral. I don't know. He is believed to have once even hit a PLO official. He's strictly professional. He has no known political ties. He may even be several people working out of a syndicate and using one code name. However, we have doubts about that. We're operating on the theory that it's only one person."

"What's his name?"

"We don't know his name. Nobody does. He deals through middlemen, and even they don't know his name. It seems he's a master of disguise, speaks several languages, not even his gender is known for certain. Yet we have no serious doubts that he is a man. Yet there are rumors..."

"What do you mean? Surely you know if the person you're after is a man or a woman."

"You will recall the situation with Yacob," the director explained. "He wasn't shot through his hotel window. That's the story we fed the press. In actuality he was shot from within his room."

"God!" the Prime Minister exclaimed. "How did the

assassin get in?''

"Allow me to explain," said the director. "Yacob's reputation as a lady's man is legendary. Our reports indicate that he apparently noticed a Negro girl in a restaurant who struck his fancy. Evidently he invited the girl to his room. After she got in, she shot him.''

"Jesus! Then the assassin is a Negro?''

"Maybe. Maybe not. As I said, he's a master of disguise.''

"What else do we know about him?'' asked the Prime Minister. Bewilderment and fatigue showed in his face.

The director said, "The girl was approximately six feet tall. That gives us an idea of the assassin's height. Unless special shoes were worn. They could make him seem taller, but not shorter. We also know his code name.''

"Well that's at least a start. What's the bugger's code name?'' Suddenly, the Prime Minister seemed invigorated.

"Pisces. The Arabs call him Al-Hut which means 'the fish.' We do not know why he has that particular code name. We are studying the possibilities however.''

The Prime Minister pondered this information for a long moment.

"Well, I want you to hook this fish, you hear me, Ben? And I don't want any cowshit out of you.''

The Prime Minister got to his feet and the director knew his appointment was over. He walked to the door, opened it and was about to depart when the temptation became more than he could bear.

"I believe,'' he said softly, "the correct expression is 'bullshit.'''

Chapter Four

The old man disembarked from the subway at 116th Street and Lenox Avenue. Slowly, painfully, he negotiated the steps from the ramp to the surface, aided by a brown, wooden cane. Halfway to the top he stopped to catch his breath. Four boys, between the ages of ten and twelve years old, rushed up behind him. They were dressed in dark suits, bow ties and each wore his hair closely cropped.

They were laughing and racing up the steps until they came, unexpectedly, upon the elderly man.

"Oh, excuse me," the largest of the group said. "We didn't see you, sir."

"That's all right, sonny. That's all right," the old man said.

"Are you okay? I mean, you're not sick or nothing, are you?"

"No, no. I'm fit as a fiddle. Just resting a bit. That's all.

You boys run along now. Run along.''

Reluctantly, the boys left. The old man pulled nervously on his white beard. Then he forged on up the stairs.

When he reached the top he looked about curiously at his surroundings. In the middle of Harlem—the world's worst social desert—was an oasis of progress. He admired the Muslim businesses for a moment, watched the serious, clean-faced Muslim men working diligently behind the counters, and the modestly attired sisters who moved about smoothly and purposefully.

The Temple was a massive, modern structure with a huge gold colored dome at the top. At the dome's apex a golden crescent and star revolved perpetually.

To the old man it was a breathtaking view. Onward he plodded until he came to a sign on the Mosque's side facing 116th Street which announced: ''Muhammad's Temple of Islam No. 7 and the University of Islam.''

The large metal door opened, seemingly by automation. But there was a Muslim brother behind it looking out through a one-way mirror.

''This way, sir.'' A dark-skinned, smiling young man in a business suit directed him to an anteroom. Several men were being frisked there.

''Is this your first visit to Muhammad's Temple?'' another young man asked.

''Yes,'' the old man replied.

''Sir, we have a search procedure,'' the man said in polite, but clipped military-like tones. ''No items such as drugs, alcohol, knives, guns or weapons of any sort are allowed inside the Temple. Would you empty your pockets please, sir?''

The old man did so. He only had a wallet, a handkerchief and an ink pen. The young man placed the items in the old man's outstretched hands. He lifted the pen, pointed it at the

41

old man and clicked it twice. Then, in swift and precise movements, he shook out the handkerchief and bent the wallet to make certain no hard objects were within. Then, with fast and smooth motions he frisked the old man. First the collar, then the lapels of his coat, then the sleeves and the coat's inner lining, now around the back and the front of the shirt, then the waistline, the zipper, the pants legs and the top of the shoes.

"Would you turn around please, sir?"

The old man did as he was directed.

"Lift one foot."

The man nearly stumbled but managed to retain his balance with the help of his cane. The man twisted the heel on his shoe. Satisfied that it wasn't a trick heel, he told the man to lift the other. He repeated the same check.

The whole procedure had taken less than thirty seconds.

The old man was then directed to a corridor. He was about to climb three flights of stairs when a large, heavyset, light skinned man said, "Don't take the stairs. Here, ride the elevator."

He pushed a button and a door slid open. They both rode the elevator to the third floor. They walked to the auditorium. The meeting was already in progress.

The assistant minister, a tall, well-built young man of brown complexion, was speaking in moderate, well-modulated tones. The assistant minister had a quick, easy smile that almost forced the audience to relax. The purpose of his short talk was to "warm up" the audience for the principal speaker.

"So, brothers and sisters, we're blessed to have Minister Farrakhan back in New York. He's just come back from an audience with the Messenger and..."

The audience broke out with spontaneous applause. "Yes sir," someone shouted.

"And we know," the assistant minister continued, "that the Honorable Elijah Muhammad gave him some wisdom that we're all very anxious to hear. If Minister Farrakhan is listening on the intercom, we'd like him to know that we're ready whenever he is."

"Yes sir," several people in the audience exclaimed.

Minutes later Minister Farrakhan entered the auditorium. All eyes turned in his direction as the minister strode, stern faced, towards the podium. He was impeccably attired in a blue suit and matching bow tie. His wavy hair was parted on the left and he appeared at least a decade younger than his forty years.

After Minister Farrakhan had been introduced and approached the rostrum, several people stood up, their hands clapping. Most of these were non-Muslim visitors who were unfamiliar with Minister Farrakhan's instructions to his congregation to refrain from such emotional outbursts.

Men were seated on the right half of the auditorium and, separated by an aisle, women occupied the left half.

As the applause thundered on, Farrakhan raised his hands in a gesture for silence. Almost instantly the auditorium became quiet.

All of Farrakhan's Sunday lectures from Muhammad's Temple No. 7 were broadcast live over WLIB radio in New York. Later they were re-aired over WBLS-FM and WWRL. In addition, he made a weekly tape, substituting for the nominal featured speaker, Elijah Muhammad, over WRVR. That tape was the nationally syndicated program, *Mr. Muhammad Speaks*.

In the role he played on behalf of the Honorable Elijah Muhammad and the Nation of Islam, Farrakhan was the successor of Minister Malcolm X and he was fast becoming the most influential Muslim in America.

Looking first at the brothers and then at the sisters, his

eyes seemingly falling upon each individual, Minister Farrakhan gave the traditional Arabic Muslim greeting: "As-Salaam-Alaikum."

"Wa-Alaikum-Salaam," the congregation thundered back.

"In the Name of Allah," began Farrakhan, "who came in the Person of Master Fard Muhammad, the One God to Whom all praise is due, the Lord of the Worlds. We thank Allah for blessing us, the Black Man and Black Woman of America, with a divine leader, a divine teacher and a divine guide in the personage of the Honorable Elijah Muhammad.

"My beloved brothers and sisters, we are very honored that you have elected to take this time out of your very busy schedules to spend a few hours with us. We don't intend to be here too long, by the help of Allah."

Mild laughter followed Farrakhan's last remark since the minister was known to speak for as long as four hours at a time.

Farrakhan continued: "Whether you have traveled from the Bronx, Brooklyn, Newark, Staten Island or Queens; wherever you may be: in Jersey City, in the Tombs, on Rikers Island, wherever you are under the sound of my voice, you are blessed by God today because you are in a position to hear the life-sustaining and life-giving message of Allah's Last Messenger, the Honorable Elijah Muhammad.

"In the first chapter of the Holy Quran, which is referred to as the seven oft-repeated verses of the Quran, there is a verse which reads like this: 'Oh Allah, guide us on the right path'. Now these are words that we speak using the tongue, the lips, the teeth, the hard palate, causing the vocal cords to vibrate to produce these sounds."

"That's right, Brother Minister," a voice sounded from the audience.

"But these are not just words coming from a man who is praying to God to guide him onto the right path," continued

44

Farrakhan pedantically. "These words are ingrained on the very nature of that person who is praying."

"Take your time, Brother Minister."

"In the very nature of the black man," Farrakhan went on, "he cries out to be guided aright. His will is to be guided aright."

"Come on with it, Brother Minister."

"Now you may wonder where we're going," said Farrakhan.

"That's what they're wondering!" agreed a brother.

"Don't wonder about it. Just follow along."

"Oh, that's heavy! Heavy!" exclaimed a light-skinned brother who occupied the front row.

The old man looked around him at the men and women in the Temple. Then he returned his gaze to Farrakhan, wondering how many of the Messenger's other ministers taught subjects out of the Quran. He remembered a time when the Quran wasn't quoted at all. Years ago only Elijah and Fard had read the Quran and others were forbidden to read it. As a carryover from those days most ministers, even now, quoted the Bible in preference to the Quran.

"...but how can you claim that you've been guided aright when you haven't even been guided into a knowledge of your own *names*."

"Yessir! That's right! Teach!"

"You have lost your true identity, your true culture, your true religion and your true *names*. Now you're Jones and James and Fish and Bear and Culpepper and McGillicuddin."

The audience applauded enthusiastically.

"Wait a minute!" Farrakhan chided. "Wait a minute! You clap too much and think too little. Let's reason it out. No, we haven't been receiving right guidance. All of that which we have acquired from the white man has not been sufficient to lift us up from the mud of civilization. Oh, I know what

45

you're thinking: 'I have my master's degree from Yale.' Dear Brother, what makes you think that the same blue-eyed devil who wouldn't *treat* you right would *teach* you right.''

"Go 'head, Brother Minister! Make it plain!''

The old man marveled over the similarities between the speaker and a young convict he'd visited in prison years ago. That young man had gone on to become internationally famous as Minister Malcolm X.

"The Honorable Elijah Muhammad, the Messenger of Allah, teaches us that the white race is a race of devils. Now, I know some of you get all hot and bothered when you hear that. Some of you love white people better than life itself. Well, Brother Farrakhan is here to let you know that Almighty God Allah has raised up in our midst the Honorable Elijah Muhammad to warn you that your white boss, your white professor, your white doctor, your white president, and yes, your white Pope, is the devil!''

"Teach! Teach!''

"If God destroyed Babylon, if He destroyed Sodom and Gommorah, what makes you think He'll spare white America?''

The old man studied every face he could see to determine the effect these words were having. It was three hours later that Minister Farrakhan reached the end of his sermon.

"In my conclusion I want you to think on this. Almighty God Allah raised up Moses to redeem the suffering Children of Israel. He raised up Hud for the 'Ad and Salih for the Thamud. Every race, every nation has had its messengers except you and I. Now, would God be just if He gave every nation a messenger but excluded us? And we're catching more hell than Israel, more than Thamud and 'Ad and far more than the Arabs? Would that be just? But, oh my beloved and beautiful black brothers and sisters, God has *not* failed! Allah has raised, for us, a messenger. He has sent, for us,

46

a warner. A warner to a people to whom no warner has come before. As it is written: 'for unto us a child is born. And unto us a son is given. And a government shall be upon his shoulders. And he shall be called wonderful counsellor, the mighty God, the everlasting father, the prince of peace.'

"That one prophesied in scripture is the Messenger of Allah, the Honorable Elijah Muhammad."

The old man left the Temple and hailed a taxi on Lenox Avenue.

"La Guardia Airport," he instructed.

Ishaq Bayan was publicly known as Isaac Payne. Long ago he'd learned that P's and B's were interchangeable, having studied etymology in college. And the name Ishaq was the Arabic equivalent of the Hebrew Isaac. He figured to attract less attention with the name with which he was born, Isaac Payne, than with his Muslim name, Ishaq Bayan. Only his close circle of associates knew of his adopted name.

The Allegheny flight landed in Boston, and Payne took a cab to his apartment at 3 Howland Drive in Roxbury.

He walked slowly up a flight of stairs. It was late and he was exhausted. But he knew sleep was not to be his to have for several more hours at least.

Payne used a key to open the door. In the living room four elderly black men waited for him.

"As-Salaam-Alaikum," Isaac greeted the men who occupied the small living room. Solemn faced, one of them said, "You're very late."

Isaac took a moment to collect himself.

"I'd like to freshen up a bit," he announced and departed for the bathroom.

Minutes later, Isaac returned to the living room where the men waited, not at all patiently.

Each of the men had a key, but it was to Isaac Payne that the apartment was leased. Whenever the meetings were designated for Payne's house, they met there in the cramped quarters. Neighbors, seeing the old men arrive, thought the old timers came together to help fight each others' loneliness by playing cards, checkers or watching TV while exchanging gossip that, sometimes, was more than a quarter of a century old.

At 65, Isaac Payne was the group's youngest member. Jacob Robb (aka Ya'qub Rabb) was 72; Joseph Malcolm (aka Yusuf Malik) was 74; Michael Solomon (aka Mikal Sulaiman), at 80, was the group's senior.

These innocent seeming oldsters were the Guardian Angels. Although in public they were church deacons, Prince Hall Masons and admired professionals, in reality each was a Muslim and each had been personally converted to the faith by the man revered as God Himself, Wallace Fard Muhammad.

During his brief period of public work in Detroit from 1930 until 1934, Fard Muhammad was known variously as W. F. Fard, Wallace D. Fard, Wallace F. Muhammad, Professor Fard, Professor Ford, and Osman Sharrieff, to name just a few.

Among the members of the Nation of Islam he is usually referred to as Master Fard Muhammad. It was he who founded the Nation of Islam and he who taught Elijah Poole his strange doctrine and gave him the name Elijah Muhammad.

The four men who formed the Guardian Angels had been among Fard's few educated followers. During Fard's three and one half years of public work, they were almost inseparable from Fard's tight inner circle.

Since Fard's departure in the early 1930s, these men had devoted themselves to secretly guiding the Nation of Islam into directions that they thought best. Even the leader, Elijah Muhammad, was unaware of their work and influence.

Soon after Fard Muhammad's own departure, these highly placed lieutenants of his vanished also. Elijah naturally thought they'd "fallen by the wayside," i.e., turned apostate along with hundreds of others who rejected his claim on the mantle of leadership.

While Elijah had only an elementary education, these four men had already obtained advanced degrees. And, at Fard's insistence, they set out to gain mastery of additional fields of study. Now, as Fard had planned, each had mastered several disciplines over the years.

Nation of Islam literature frequently mentions twenty-four scientists, imams or angels who had the ability to "write history in advance." It was the hope of the Guardian Angels to fulfill the role of the twenty-four scientists. To them, the number twenty-four had esoteric meaning. It meant the full scope of human knowledge in both the physical and spiritual realms. To them universality was symbolized by the number twelve. The earth passed through twelve months and there were twelve houses in the zodiac. But human life manifested on two planes: physical and spiritual. So the complete understanding was symbolically called twenty-four. To them, the twenty-four scientists represented any number of people who had gained universal understanding on both planes.

In the forty years since Fard Muhammad's departure, none of the Guardian Angels had seen him. Yet each of them had received mysterious messages at critical periods in the Nation of Islam's history. They were certain that these messages had been sent by Master Fard Muhammad.

Master Fard Muhammad had told them to "write the history of the Black Man in advance." And they'd spent years trying to arrive at methods of accurately predicting world events. They had attempted to devise mathematical methods for determining the moods of people and to calculate what actions those moods would create.

Finally, they arrived at the understanding that the true meaning of Fard's instruction was for them to gain control over the reins of power so that they could bring about events according to their plan. By controlling the contingencies, they could accurately predict what would occur. Because they would make it occur.

Fard meant that they should devise a Master Plan (symbolically called a Mother Plan) and that they should cause events to occur that would further that plan.

It was unanimously agreed among them that the American black man would be the principal mover of the international black community in the years to come, owing to his superior educational and economic opportunities. Additionally, his unique history so paralleled that of Biblical Israel that he had a scriptural base for leadership.

It was also agreed that the Nation of Islam would become the dominant influence upon Black America. So, logically, it became imperative to first gain control of the Nation of Islam so that direction of world black society could gradually come into their hands. A wheel (Nation of Islam) within a wheel (world black community).

Although Elijah initially worried that some of the more educated Muslims would seize his power, over the years he gradually became less concerned with that fear. He practically forgot about all the highly intelligent men who had comprised a vital part of Fard's inner circle.

They'd begun their plan to usurp power during the late 1940s prior to the Nation's rapid growth under the eloquent oratory of Malcolm X.

The Angels had devised a plan to send their hand-picked students into the major Temples in subordinate but significant roles. Seldom did the "Five Percenters," as these agents were called, accept attention-attracting posts like minister or captain of a Temple. Most often they were secretaries or assistant secretaries, as this gave them access to all vital information. They were the people who could be counted on to get the job done. They worked tirelessly and were careful not to pose the least threat to their superiors' positions or egos. They were the silent workers, the "good soldiers," who were first to arrive at the Temple and last to depart.

Eventually, almost every powerful person in the Nation had at least one assistant who was a Five Percenter. The Supreme Captain leaned heavily on a Five Percenter; the former National Minister, Malcolm X, relied on "a very capable brother" who was a Five Percenter; the aide to the National Secretary was a Five Percenter; the regional ministers in Washington, D.C., Chicago, Atlanta and Los Angeles were all provided hard-working secretaries, assistant ministers or lieutenants who were actually Five Percenters.

When Malcolm departed from the Nation of Islam, a new Five Percenter was sent to assist his replacement in New York.

Other powerful Temples such as those located in Philadelphia, Detroit, Newark, Boston, Baltimore and New Orleans were also infiltrated by Five Percenters.

Soon, the "laborers" (Temple officials) were content to strut about powerfully while leaving much of the real responsibility and authority to their assistants. And these never-complaining aides encouraged the laborers toward more and more sloth and moral degradation with a knowing smile or an understanding wink at some moral infraction.

As their power grew, the Five Percenters might suggest something like: "Being the Minister puts so much pressure on a brother that sometimes he has to let off some steam." Such suggestions were usually followed by the sending of an attractive sister to the minister or captain to request "private counselling on a pressing domestic problem." Nearly always the laborers were thus compromised.

Eventually suggestions were made that the laborers take larger salaries than was officially permitted.

"A poverty-stricken minister can't do the Messenger much good." Or, "How do you expect the Lost-Founds to see their success in Islam when the Minister himself is poor? Now, if you had a Cadillac..."

Or, at times, the argument would go: "You deserve better, Brother Minister. Allah has promised us money, good homes and friendship in all walks of life. The Messenger has already told us to do something for self. If we arranged for a small portion of the Number Two Poor Treasury to go to the Minister's Maintenance Fund instead of sending it to Chicago..."

The greed led to criminal misconduct in several major cities, Philadelphia being most noted among them. In some cities the word "Muslim" became synonymous with "gangster."

The "Angels" decided that regional rivalries were advantageous to their plan, so ill feelings were bred between the major power brokers by the Five Percenters.

In Chicago, high officials were told to beware of Minister Farrakhan, because he was trying to take over the Nation. In New York, the minister was warned to watch out for the officials in Chicago because they were jealous of his popularity. The ministers of the various Temples were warned of the expansionist designs of neighboring ministers.

Each move the laborers made was dutifully reported to the Guardian Angels. Only thrice was their Master Plan imperiled.

The first occurred when Malcolm X spoke with Oliver Muhammad, an old follower of Fard who lived in New Orleans. Oliver knew of Fard's alternate plan and dropped the entire scenario on an incredulous Malcolm.

At first Malcolm tried to disregard the words of the elderly

Muslim. But his mind was constantly discomfited by what he'd heard.

When Malcolm finally moved to investigate, his activities were reported to the Angels. Immediately efforts were made to neutralize Malcolm.

As it was known that a small rift had already begun to develop between Malcolm and Elijah, it was decided that it was best to widen that crack by playing on the envy of Malcolm which was abundant in Chicago, and by playing on the Messenger's own fears that his students would one day outstrip him.

When Kennedy was assassinated, Elijah cancelled a scheduled speaking appearance in New York out of regard for the slain president. Malcolm, concerned that the New York Mosque would lose thousands of dollars spent in advertising and for the rental of the hall, asked the Messenger to permit him to speak in his stead. Elijah was unhappy with this suggestion but, when Malcolm persisted, he relented.

"I still have bad feelings about this," the Messenger told Malcolm.

Malcolm was instructed to refrain from commenting on the President's death regardless of the circumstances. And should anyone ask a question about Kennedy, Malcolm was instructed to reply, "No comment."

During the main lecture Malcolm adhered to the Messenger's orders. But following the lecture was a question-and-answer period and during this period someone asked his reaction to President Kennedy's assassination.

Malcolm replied that it was "a case of chickens coming home to roost. And being an old country boy myself, chickens coming home to roost never made me sad, they always made me glad."

The press had a field day with Malcolm's remarks. And the Five Percenters in Chicago—some of whom were now confidants of Elijah himself—urged the ailing Messenger to punish him severely.

Elijah was reluctant to move against his best minister. But he eventually acquiesced to his advisors' wishes and "silenced" Malcolm for ninety days. In addition to being silenced, Malcolm later learned that he was suspended from the Nation of Islam for that period.

Malcolm gave his ear to his own Five Percenter advisors. They told him that he didn't have to take that kind of treatment from anyone, not even from the Messenger. It was he, Malcolm, who had crossed the continent building Temples. Without him, no one would even know Elijah Muhammad existed.

After his ninety-day suspension had expired and Elijah still refused to re-admit him, Malcolm took his advisors' counsel. He left the Nation of Islam to form his own organization, the Muslim Mosque, Inc. He also founded a non-religious entity, the Organization of Afro-American Unity, which was styled after the international organization founded by Kwame Nkrumah, the Organization of African Unity.

But during his travels across the globe Malcolm came to suspect that events had been guided by an invisible hand. After his trip to Mecca he reflected upon the conversation he'd had with Oliver Muhammad.

After much soul-searching he decided to seek a conference with the Honorable Elijah Muhammad. By this time, Malcolm had several very definite differences with Elijah's theological doctrine. But he placed the unity of the movement above their ideological variances.

Elijah was of the opinion that the prodigal son was finally returning to his rightful home. He saw Malcolm's secret overture as a fulfillment of scripture. He was close to "permitting" his dissident minister to meet with him.

Correspondingly, Malcolm toned down his attacks upon

the leader. The attempts on Malcolm's life were no longer from the Nation of Islam, but from the United States government.

Elijah was prepared to summon Malcolm immediately, but one of his advisors persuaded him to postpone the meeting until the evening prior to the annual Saviour's Day convention. And if a reconciliation was made, Malcolm would announce his "return home" at the national convention.

Malcolm, for years, had been touted as Elijah's successor. But the Guardian Angels had already committed themselves to making sure that Master Fard Muhammad's selection, more than thirty years ago, would rise to power. They feared that Malcolm's return might upset that ascension.

Malcolm never got to see Muhammad. Less than a week before the convention, on February 21, 1965, Malcolm was gunned down in an execution that was hastily arranged by the Guardian Angels.

Later, one of the Five Percenters named Clarence 13X defected and started his own cult which he also named the Five Percenters.

When Clarence declared himself "Supreme Allah" and began attracting hundreds of followers from prisons and reformatories in the New York area, the Guardian Angels decided to give him some assistance. One of his "followers" arranged a meeting to "prove beyond all doubt that Clarence, the Father, is in fact the Supreme Allah.

He gathered a group of believers around Clarence and screamed: "I know you are Allah. You are He who lives and dies not!" Then he emptied a revolver into Clarence's body. Clarence died on the spot.

The last threat to the Angels' scheme came from the "Son of Thunder," Minister James Shabazz of Newark. He'd been a minister under Elijah for more than twenty-five years and he knew something was happening to the Nation from hidden, external forces. But he made the mistake of discussing his fears and suspicions with a very close friend. That friend was a Five Percenter.

When James had collected enough data to approach Elijah, he was assassinated in his own driveway by agents of the Guardian Angels.

"I think we're making a big mistake," Isaac Payne announced to his colleagues. "That's why I had to go to New York and listen to Louis myself. The boy has definitely developed. If you give him a few more years, he'll be able to lead."

"That is precisely what we don't want," said Jacob Robb. "We all know Louis, but he's not the one the Savior chose. You know that. But if we let him go on much longer, the people will demand that he take over after Elijah. It'll be next to impossible for Wallace to get in. We cannot permit that. We are committed to carrying out the will of the Saviour. Besides, Wallace is ready *now*. He doesn't require any more years to get ready. Farrakhan must be removed from consideration."

"Ya'qub," said Isaac, "Louis is only forty years old. He has served the cause faithfully and tirelessly. It seems such a waste to eliminate someone who has such potential. 'Allah loves not the wasters,' if I may quote the Quran."

"And if we fail to make certain that Wallace gets the position, that, I suggest to you, would be the greatest of all wastes," countered Jacob.

Jacob went on: "The Saviour himself chose Wallace. He taught Clara the proper way to raise him, what to teach him and what to feed him. His most formative years were spent in accord with the Saviour's instructions. The boy is a genius. And you say that Louis is spiritually inclined. I dare say not a man alive is as spiritually inclined or as theologically enlightened as Wallace.''

"I don't trust him, Ya'qub,'' Isaac stated. "He's always in and out, never settled. If he can't settle his own life, how can he stabilize the Nation? And all of that Arab motif. He's too much in love with the Arab style, Arab culture. He has no loyalty to his father. Whenever I look up I see that he's in this or that faraway country doing God knows what. What's he up to? No, I don't trust him at all.''

Jacob said, "Has it occurred to you that he has developed so precisely because he has been free to travel and to broaden his scope? And what you erroneously think to be disloyalty to his father is merely a gifted young man exercising his own God-given intelligence, viewing the world with his own eyes. Because Wallace is Elijah's son he enjoys the personal security to disagree, at least subjectively. But Farrakhan and the others are so afraid of being at variance with the Messenger that they stifle their own growth by forcing themselves to concur with Elijah no matter how absurd the statement or how counter-productive the deed.''

"Enough! Both of you have said enough!'' Michael Solomon, the unofficial dean of the Guardian Angels spoke up.

"Maybe we don't have to liquidate Farrakhan. Maybe, but I doubt it, he'll accept a subordinate position to Wallace. It's a gamble, but there is an alternative. I agree that in another few years Farrakhan will be the de facto leader. Right now, should a vote be taken, he'd win running away.

"However, the Nation of Islam is not a democratic society and quite a few members are not yet secure with Farrakhan. We have learned that, during a crisis, most members still look toward the royal family, Elijah's sons, for guidance. This they have always done.

"There is but one way for us to assure Wallace's ascension and still spare Farrakhan's life. But we must all agree.

Otherwise we proceed as planned."

The old man seemed exhausted from his speech, but after a moment's rest he went on to outline a plan.

Minutes later he was finished.

Isaac, as he was so concerned with sparing Farrakhan, would have to locate and select the proper "operator." He continued, receiving an opinion from Yusuf Malik on the "psychological impact of this endeavor and the probable reactions of the membership." They traded insights for hours.

Finally, they voted.

Jacob spoke. "Then we are all agreed. It is unanimous." He sighed, and for a moment it seemed that he would cry.

When Yusuf Malik spoke, tears reddened his eyes. "In the Name of Allah, I hope we realize what we've done. May God have mercy upon our souls."

Jacob Robb said, "The unthinkable has become unavoidable. We have just decided to murder the Messenger of Allah."

Chapter Five

Eric Schofield had just completed a taping of *The Larry Anderson Show,* a popular daytime talk show that was challenging Phil Donahue's daytime supremacy. This was the last of a score of appearances he'd made since the publication of *Lovetown.*

Tracey Bivens waited for him in the studio audience. Eric, relieved to be free of his obligation to push the book, barely resisted a sudden urge to embrace her.

"How'd I do?" he asked.

"You were wonderful," she answered. "It almost seemed like you were enjoying yourself."

He laughed, draped an arm over her shoulder and said, "To be frank, I have to admit that I was."

A few people who were in the studio audience came up to Eric and requested his autograph. Eric still hadn't adjusted to his budding celebrity status and hesitated momentarily before complying.

"Tell me something, Mr. Schofield," a woman asked, "is your *Lovetown* just a report on the inner workings of Motown?"

"Well, ma'am, *Lovetown* is set in Philadelphia while Motown, last time I checked, is a Detroit-Hollywood based company," Schofield said.

"But," she persisted, "your characters seem a lot like the people at Motown. Seems like you just moved the location to Philadelphia. The owner of Lovetown Record Corporation seems identical to Berry Gordy. Your talented but trouble-plagued singer from Washington seems very similar to Marvin Gaye. Only you have him trying out for the 76ers instead of the Detroit Lions. Then, at the end, you have the mob taking over the company. And plenty of people claim that's what happened to Motown."

"Honey, you have such a marvelous imagination you should think about writing a novel yourself. Here's my agent, maybe she can help you. Nice talking with you."

He practically pushed Tracey into the woman. But before escaping the inquisitive woman's questions he whispered to Tracey, "Be at your house after nine tonight, okay?"

She knew he was using her to get away from the woman and also trying to duck other autograph seekers. But she didn't mind too much. He'd been such a darling to agree to do all the shows they'd arranged.

"Okay," she whispered back.

Since the beginning of the promotional campaign she and Eric had had little time together alone. And under the pressure of the campaign they'd pretty much fallen back into their old buddy-buddy relationship.

But Eric's whispered request to see her tonight signaled a shift in his immediate interests and suggested more exciting things to follow. But then maybe he just wanted to watch a game or something on television. Eric Schofield was a hard dude to predict.

Schofield trotted across the parking lot toward his new Mercedes roadster. With the heady experience of near stardom, he'd given in and allowed himself the opulence of a new car.

He was especially happy now that he'd received news that *Lovetown* was going to be on the *Times'* fiction bestseller list. Things couldn't be going much better, he thought.

"Mr. Schofield!" a man's voice called.

Eric stopped and turned, trying to mask his irritation at being stopped by another autograph seeker.

"I really liked the show," the man said as he approached Eric. Eric noticed that he was elderly, and the white beard which starkly contrasted his very black face caught Eric's attention.

Hoping to get the autograph signing over with as quickly as possible Eric extracted his pen.

"Thank you, sir," he said waiting for the man to produce an autograph book or something.

"I found particularly interesting your remarks in reference to Vietnam," the man was saying.

When's this joker gonna bring out his autograph book so I can cut out? thought Eric.

"Mister, how would you like me to sign it?" Eric asked the man.

"I beg your pardon?"

"The autograph. How do you want it? You do want an autograph, don't you?"

The man laughed briefly as though he was laughing as much at himself as at what Schofield had said.

"Well, I was hoping we could chat a bit. You see..."

"Sir, I'm really in a hurry and I can't talk right now. If you'll excuse..."

61

"I don't wish to detain you, but it's just that some of your statements about your Vietnam tour were inaccurate, and . . ."

"Mister," Eric said testily, "exactly what is it you're trying to say?"

"Mr. Schofield, you said you were involved with demolitions in Vietnam. And I know that you did do some work in that area. But, really, that was a mere fraction of your activities. I happen to know for certain that you were in espionage."

Eric stared at the man in surprise. Nobody was supposed to know the nature of his work in "special operations."

"Who are you?" Eric asked at length. An icy edge came over his voice.

"May I get a lift? I've never ridden in a car like yours before. I should think it will be nice. Besides, a parking lot seems hardly the proper place for gentlemen to converse."

"We don't have a thing to talk about, buddy. So if you have something to say you better spit it out now. Else you'll be here talking to yourself."

The man pulled on his beard. "If you prefer that we discuss this under such circumstances, so be it." The man paused. "I want you to kill someone for me."

"You what?" Eric yelled. Something was terribly wrong. People didn't just walk up to you and ask you to kill someone. He had representatives, carefully selected, on four continents who were paid to negotiate with prospective clients. Eric never even saw his clients and they never knew who he was.

"Mister, I don't have the slightest idea what you're talking about," Eric said.

"Mr. Schofield, I am not a fool and I know fully well who and what you are. I know all of your middlemen and I elected to bypass them. This is a situation that is, if I may borrow one of the phrases popular among men in your trade, for your eyes only.''

Eric forced out a laugh. "Buster, you got the wrong man. If you want a hit man, you better check out the Cosa Nostra or somebody." He turned to walk away.

"Why don't you cease this facade? I know who you are. I know quite a lot about you, in fact. I know about that little job you pulled for Qaddafi last year. I know about the dock leader who disappeared. I know about the project you handled in Mozambique for the Republic of South Africa. When you did that work in Guinea Bissau in '73 I thought you'd retire. But you are either a very greedy man or a thrill seeker because you have still not retired. Now, do you choose to persist in your rather juvenile deception or are you prepared to talk business, Mr. Schofield? Or should I call you Pisces?"

"What'd you call me?" Eric was stunned.

"You know damned well what I called you. Pisces. Or, as the Arabs say, Al-Hut—The Fish.''

At this point Eric stepped forward on his left foot and with his right he swept the old man, knocking him to the concrete. With a cat's swiftness Eric was upon him, pressing him roughly to the ground.

"You move and I'll snap your neck," Schofield breathed. The old man lay still. Eric ran his hands over the man's body. He found no weapons, no recording equipment, no microphones.

"Mister, if you're bullshitting me . . ."

"This is no joke, young man. I would think a quarter of a million dollars is a serious sum."

"A quarter of a million?"

"Please let me up. You have determined that I am not armed."

Eric allowed the man to rise.

"I'm not saying that I know a thing about what you're asking, and definitely not that I would do it; but, out of curiosity, who do you want to get rid of?"

Eric knew his words sounded amateurish, but he had to put some protection on himself in case he was being set up. There might be hidden microphones somewhere in the parking lot.

It was a good thing Larry Anderson was taping another segment of his program at the moment, or the parking lot would have been full of people leaving the studio. As it was, it was still deserted.

"Do you have a Bible?" the old man asked.

"No, but I guess I can get one, why?"

"When you do, turn to the Book of Malachi. Read chapter four, verses five and six. Then you will know."

"How shall I reach you?" Eric asked.

"You shan't. But I'll contact you in a few days," said Isaac Payne.

Chapter Six

Tracey looked at Eric who was laying beside her. Even with the lights out she could tell that he wasn't sleeping. Something was wrong, she could tell. Even in their lovemaking he'd seemed distracted.

If he was bored with her, he shouldn't have come to see her. She didn't have a chain around his neck. Their relationship wasn't like that. So if he wanted to go back to their former relationship and drop the eroticism, that was cool with her. She liked him a lot, but it wasn't as if she was madly in love with him or anything.

"Tracey, do you have a Bible?" Eric whispered in the dark.

"A what? Did I hear you right?"

"Uh huh. You got a Bible?"

Now she *was* worried. Was Eric turning into some sort of Jesus freak or something? She'd heard that people flipped over and got born again very rapidly. Maybe he was on a guilt trip or something because of his romantic dallyings.

"Yes, I have one. Why?"

"Get it," he said.

Though she didn't care for his commanding tone she decided now wasn't the time to bicker over his periodic chauvinism. She got up from the bed and walked, nude, to the bookshelf in the living room.

She came back with a large family Bible.

"This was my mother's gift to me," she said turning on the lights. "A high school graduation present. Daddy bought me a car. Mom gave me a Bible. I made very good use of Dad's present. I haven't used Mom's yet. Until now."

It still looked new, a verification of Tracey's remark.

"Turn to the Book of Malachi," Eric ordered. His voice was filled with impatience.

"Yessir, your majesty," she said sarcastically. She hoped he didn't take this commanding officer bit too much further, or she'd have to let some of the air out of his sails. It never failed. Give a nigger a little pussy and he thought he owned you.

She searched the alphabetical listing of Books and found Malachi.

"Got it, General Custer." He seemed to pick up on her thinly veiled irritation and his tone was noticeably more soft when he asked, "Would you read chapter four, verses five and six, please?"

"Boy, if Mom could see me now." She turned to the requested section and began to read.

"Behold," she read aloud, "I will send you Elijah the prophet before the coming of the great and dreadful day of the Lord. And he shall turn the heart of the fathers to the children, and the heart of the children to their fathers, lest I come and smite the earth with a curse."

66

Tracey glanced at Eric. His mouth hung open and his eyes were stretched wide as saucers. His breathing became more rapid and his body shuddered for a brief moment. So brief that it was almost imperceptible.

She said, "Eric, what's the matter?"

He didn't answer. Instead he reached for her and she, just a little frightened, came into his arms. She hugged him tightly. She felt his body shiver again and she patted him softly on the back.

Some time ago he had told her of a friend of his who was a professional boxer. Every night before a fight he needed someone to hold him like a baby. It was a great human paradox. The killer in the ring needed cuddling the night prior to the great violence. Then, shamed by his former weakness, the fighter is that much more vicious in the ring. That continuing unity of opposites was the basis for the dualism, the yin and yang principle, the Marxist theory called dialectical materialism, as well as one of the meanings of the astrological symbol Pisces.

Eric, she remembered, was a Pisces.

The director of MOSSAD walked briskly into Prime Minister Uri Moshe's office.

The Prime Minister looked up from a stack of papers wearily.

"What is it, Benjamin? As you can see, I'm extremely busy."

The director was well aware of the extent of the Prime Minister's workload. He also knew the nature of his toils. The Prime Minister was fighting for his political life. In one week the Moshe government could conceivably face a no confidence vote which would mark the end of his short stay in power.

"Mr. Prime Minister, I have been informed that Saleem

Mannan has been captured. Thought you'd like to know."

"You're damned right I want to know. Jeez! We just chopped off George Habash's right arm."

George Habash was the head of a more radical wing of the PLO, the Popular Front for the Liberation of Palestine. Saleem Mannan was his alter ego. On paper, Mannan held no position in the PLO hierarchy. In reality, he was Habash's most trusted adviser, co-planner of terrorist attacks and sometime coordinator of the more complex and urgent strikes against Israel and her allies. Habash's every decision was known to Saleem Mannan. Now he was not far from Tel Aviv in Israeli custody.

"How did this quail happen to fall into our hands?" asked the Prime Minister.

"Well, there was a night raid into Lebanon and..."

"Say no more. I'm in enough trouble with the softies, the so-called doves, over Lebanon already. Benjamin, you *know* I can't afford this."

"Officially, he was captured trying to cross the border into Israel, carrying explosives."

"That'll never stick. Once word gets out about us crossing into Lebanon..." The Prime Minister was furious.

"Word won't get out. You see, no one knows we were there. Not a single gunshot was fired. Good old Saleem had sneaked out of camp to pick up a girl for his boss. Habash isn't Muslim, but a lot of his men expect him to keep the tenets of their faith. So Habash has to move quietly. Saleem often goes out to pick up Habash's favorite girl friend. Our informers notified us, and we plucked him quietly and bloodlessly and brought him to Israel."

The Prime Minister grunted. The director accepted that as congratulations, albeit begrudging ones.

"Why all the interest in Saleem Mannan all of a sudden, Ben?"

"We understand he's been fishing lately," replied the director.

"Fishing?" The Prime Minister felt he'd missed something. Then he remembered. "Oh, you mean he's connected with . . ."

"Yes, sir," said the director. "It is our understanding that Saleem Mannan once contracted the services of Al-Hut, the Pisces."

Miranda Schofield had finished packing the Cokes, franks, sandwiches and charcoal that would be needed for tomorrow's picnic. Herb, her husband, would take everything out to the station wagon in the morning.

She quietly checked on her two grandchildren and saw that they were soundly sleeping. She was keeping the kids, Michael and Terry, while her daughter, Yvonne, vacationed in France with her husband Richard for two weeks.

Looking after the children periodically was a task she enjoyed. But they were so active that she was glad she didn't have that pleasure too often. If a pleasure remains, it won't remain a pleasure. Those kids never failed to leave her exhausted.

They were sweet kids really. Terry was a rather gamine little elf of eight who tried diligently to keep up with her ten-year-old brother whom she idolized. If the game was football, she was on Michael's team. If Michael decided to climb trees, there was Terry climbing up behind him.

So energetic were they that Charlene, her next door neighbor whom everyone called Charlie, insisted that she come along to the picnic to keep an extra eye on the children. French Creek, where they were going, was full of forests, had a large lake, and all sorts of small animals inhabited its wooden regions. Michael and Terry were sure to be lured into the woods in pursuit of some animal.

The children would have little difficulty eluding their grandparents, but Charlie felt she could stay within a reasonable distance of them.

It was after midnight and she wondered if she should try to call Eric again. She'd been calling him all day, with no success. She lived in Morton, Pennsylvania, minutes away from Sharon Hill, yet she saw her son so seldom it seemed as if they were continents apart. If it weren't for the TV shows on which her son was starting to appear frequently, she'd probably forget what he looked like. Yes, she'd call him. It just wasn't right for a mother to go months without seeing her son. Especially when he lived so close by.

She dialed his number. After four rings he answered.

"Hey, Mammasita!" he yelled. "How you been? I ain't seen you in *decades*. You musta been duckin' me."

"Oh hush, boy. I've been calling you for days. Aren't you ever home?"

Eric smiled. Seldom did his mother refer to his apartment as "home." She usually called it "that place." Maybe now, after all these years, she accepted the fact that his "home" was not there with them anymore. Or at least that he had another "home" too.

"Mom, I've been super busy. I've been meaning to call you for weeks, but you know . . . lotta stuff kept coming up. Hey! I been on TV. Did you see me?"

"Yes, I saw you a few times. You did well. But you looked awful. So skinny. Don't you eat anything other than Gino's junk food? But the way you keep popping up on television, that book of yours must really be jumping."

Eric laughed at her expression. "Yes, Mom. It's 'jumping.'" He laughed again. "It jumped on the best seller lists recently."

"You know I haven't even read it yet? I'm ashamed."

"Aw, Mom. You're not interested in the kind of music

I write about. Only thing that turns you on is James Cleveland, Mahalia Jackson and those kind of people. I'm sure you'd have little interest in the main subject of *Lovetown*. You've never forgiven the Staples Singers for switching over to rock and roll.''

"Indeed I haven't! It's awful! They should be ashamed!''

"See? Look at you. By the way, Mom, how's cabbage head?''

Miranda stifled a chuckle. "Eric, I won't have you referring to your father like that.'' She hoped her voice sounded stern over the phone.

"Okay, okay,'' Eric said. Then he broke into laughter and, after a moment, Miranda laughed right along with him.

Their conversations were usually like that. He always did everything he could to humorously assail all her ethics. And she, protesting, would laugh anyway. She knew Eric loved his father, but he enjoyed poking fun at him just to see her get riled up.

"Hey Mom. How's Yvonne?''

"Vonnie's in France.''

"Oh yeah? Damn. I mean darn. I didn't know.''

"You don't know anything because you're never here and you never call. That's why I'm calling you now. I'm looking after Michael and Terry. All of us are going to French Creek tomorrow and I want you to come along.''

"I wish I could, Mom. But I have to...''

"You have to do nothing! You make time for everything and everybody but your own family. Well, that's going to halt. You be here at seven o'clock sharp.''

"Mom, look. I really have some important research to do.''

"You just postpone your important research and spend some time with your important family. That's final.''

"Aw, Mom.''

"Aw nothing. Seven o'clock. You hear?"

"Oh, all right. Damn!"

"I beg your pardon?"

"I said 'darn.'"

"Besides, Eric, Charlie should have someone about the same age for company," Miranda said.

"Who's Charlie?"

"You remember, one of Vonnie's friends. Charlene Cox. Lives next door."

"You mean that skinny girl who went away to some funny named college?"

"Slippery Rock University."

"Yeah, that's it. What's she coming for?"

"She volunteered to help Dad and me keep an eye on Michael and Terry. You know how active they are. She was afraid they might run somewhere and we'd be too slow to keep up. She didn't say that, of course. But I know that's what she was thinking. Sweet girl. And she hardly could be called skinny anymore. She's really very pretty."

"Aw, come off it. You're just trying to make me want to come without having to force me."

"Well, see for yourself. But it won't do you any good. She's engaged."

Michael and Charlie had teamed up against Terry and Eric for a game of touch football on French Creek's sandy beach.

Eric played quarterback and Terry hiked the ball to him. She ran as fast as her little legs could carry her, trying to dash past Michael, her defender. Charlie rushed in, trying to tag Eric who easily eluded her lunges.

"Throw it, Uncle Eric! Throw it!" Terry screamed as she managed to get past her brother. Eric lobbed a soft pass that sailed over Michael's hands and hit Terry squarely upon her chest. The ball bounced off her chest and hung suspended in midair for a second, which was enough time for Michael to intercept it and run furiously toward the opposite "goal line" (an imaginary point beyond a beach trash can which was the marker).

Charlie skillfully blocked Eric who was trying to reach the speedy sprinter to prevent a touchdown. But, on the strength of Charlene's block, Mike sailed past Eric and scored. He kneeled down in the imaginary end zone and rolled the ball as if he were shooting craps. Harold Carmichael and the other Eagles were famous for doing the same thing after touchdowns.

Michael screamed, "John Outlaw!" in celebration of his feat. Outlaw was his favorite defensive back on the Eagles.

Eric smiled proudly at his nephew's prowess and his cute imitation of the pros. "He's good, isn't he?" he said to Charlie.

"As much as he practices in the backyard, I bet he'll become an All Star," she replied.

"In the NFL it's called All-Pro," he said.

Terry walked dejectedly toward them. Sadly, she said, "I'm sorry I missed it, Uncle Eric."

Eric picked her up and tossed her effortlessly in the air. "Don't worry 'bout a thing, pretty baby. Next time you'll catch it like Tommy MacDonald."

She giggled in delight although she hadn't the slightest notion of who Tommy MacDonald was. She was just glad her uncle wasn't mad at her. Michael always hollered at her when she missed a pass. Before they could get the next play off, Miranda called informing them that lunch was ready.

The meal was on a wooden table, everything except the Cokes, which Miranda had forgotten to take out of the ice. Eric took out a Coke for everyone. He tossed Charlie hers, but she missed it. Imitating Terry, she said, "I'm sorry I missed it, Uncle Eric."

They laughed.

A couple of hours later, after the food had settled, Miranda allowed the children to go into the water, providing they didn't go too far out.

Herb rested contentedly on a hammock he'd tied between two large trees and listened to a Dodgers-Phillies game on a transistor radio. Occasionally he'd blurt out, "God-a-mighty!" when the Dodgers either failed to score or allowed the Phillies to do so. Herb was an old Dodger fan ("They had the guts to hire Jackie Robinson, didn't they?") and hated the Phillies with a passion ("They were the last team to pick up a colored player...and look how they treated Richie Allen").

Miranda sat with her bare feet propped on a hassock and knitted a sweater for Terry to wear when school started in September.

Charlie and Eric and been posted on the beach by Miranda to watch Michael and Terry to make sure they didn't stray too far. They shared an immense beach towel and listened to the sounds emanating from Charlie's plastic, portable eight track cassette player.

Eric watched the soft waves rippling past the children splashing about in the lake. The lake was completely encircled by a deep forest. The simmering stoves brought to his nostrils the various scents of recently completed meals.

Herb and Miranda often brought Eric and Yvonne here when they were kids, and laying there watching his sister's offspring caused a wave of nostalgia to spread over Eric. Where, he wondered, had all those years gone?

"Have you ever met the Isley Brothers?" asked Charlene, breaking off his thoughts.

"Yeah. Several times. When I was researching *Sweet Soul Music*," said Eric.

"How about Stevie?"

74

"A few times. Now, he's something else. He's still just a kid. Can you imagine what he's gonna be like when he's forty or fifty? He may eclipse Beethoven. The guy's constantly experimenting and perfecting his art. Never satisfied, always reaching for more."

"What made you decide to start writing about music?" she asked.

"Well, I never considered myself a writer of anything. When I was in Nam one of my buddies was a jazz musician. He got me to start really listening to the records, the strings, the instruments, you know, whether the players were really down or not. After that," he continued, "I always listened to music on a deeper level. I mean, like, I still popped my fingers and jammed like everybody else, you know. But when I could snatch a few minutes of solitude I used to listen to records on a more analytical level."

"How did the writing come about?" asked Charlie.

The children were plunging their hands into the water trying to catch something. "It went right through my hand," he heard Terry shriek. Eric recalled how he and Yvonne used to wade in the same water and try, vainly, to catch minnows bare handed.

"I started asking my lady to send me music magazines. I had her track down all of them she could find. I had subscriptions to every major rock and roll, soul and jazz magazine. I noticed that some of the rock and roll mags were putting out some heavy stuff on white artists. But they treated black artists like a frivolous side issue. I mean, like all our superstars—Aretha, Curtis Mayfield, the Temps, even Miles—were non-entities, and that infuriated me because I knew they were putting out some quality shit."

Without forewarning he smacked her buttocks sharply.

"Ow! What...?"

He laughed. "A giant mosquito was about to bite your

75

derriere. You'd look awful strange scratching your ass all day. He would have bit right through that flimsy bikini material."

"Maybe I'd prefer the itch to the pain I've got now," she said, pouting.

"You want I should rub the pain away?" he smirked.

"Go 'head, boy," she said pushing him away. "Finish telling me about your work."

"You really wanna hear this stuff?"

"Yes, I find this 'stuff' most interesting. Now will you go on?"

She changed the tapes. Now "Ebony Woman" by Billy Paul played.

"Okay. So I was reading the black magazines too. Of them all, the only one that was worth shit—in terms of being deeply into the music—was *Downbeat*, but they specialized in jazz, and only a few people, percentage wise, were knowledgeable of jazz."

"I disagree with that," Charlene interrupted.

"That's 'cause you're on the campus. Jazz has always been popular among college kids because y'all wanna seem deep and sophisticated. But soon as y'all leave school, it's back to James Brown and Solomon Burke."

"Solomon who?"

"Never mind. Okay, a sizeable minority are jazz enthusiasts. Will you accept that?"

"Maybe. How sizeable?"

"How about a half of one percent," he said mischievously.

"Just go ahead with the story," she said, exasperated.

"Yeah. Anyway, the other black magazines were so juvenile that they were ridiculous. Like, I got embarrassed just reading that shit. Take for example Curtis Mayfield's *Back to the World* that came out after *Superfly*. *Superfly* was a masterpiece. *Back to the World* wasn't shit. But black writers tripped all over themselves praising that creative flop. And then, if you read some of that crap, you'd get the impression that every black star was just a darling of a person—charitable, hard working, a 'wonderful mother,' whatever the fuck that is, a loving husband, on the rise, not conceited—'her stardom still surprises and puzzles her'—sweet, sensitive and caring. Now I know everybody can't be all that. Man, that stuff nauseated me.''

"Yes, I can see that it does,'' Charlie said.

"Excuse me,'' said Eric. "I was getting kind of carried away, wasn't I.''

"I think you scared all the fish away,'' she said. "Speaking of fish, you think we should call in our two minnows now? They've been in the water for quite a while now.''

"Naw. Let 'em hang out a little while longer. They'll come out when they start getting cold and uncomfortable. Or bored.''

"Okay then. Back to you. Your indignation with the black press for their reportage is documented. How did you happen to usurp center stage?'' Charlie asked.

"I kept complaining, you know, after I got back from Vietnam. And my lady got sick of hearing me complain and complain . . .''

"Does your lady have a name?'' inquired Charlie.

"Oh, yeah. Her name is . . . was Laura.''

"Was?''

"Yeah. She's dead.''

"Oh, Eric, I'm sorry! I didn't . . .''

"Aw, don't worry about it. Been a long time now.'' But the pain, still raw, remained etched in his face. After a moment he went on. "So it got to the point where I was always telling Laura how I'd write a particular article. I'd be all the time second guessing the writers and criticizing and all. So, I musta got on her nerves 'cause one night she jumped outta bed and went and got a pad and pen. She said, 'Okay, Mr. Know-It-All. *You* write the review.' I had been complaining over a review on the first album by Barry White. And all everybody kept writing about was how much he sounded like Isaac Hayes and how he was imitating Isaac."

"Well, wasn't he?" said Charlene.

"Hell no! Well, he rapped in the beginning of some songs like Ike, but their music is radically different. Ike is a heavy horn man. He's got a strong brass section. His music is real masculine. Those horns and later the guitar just keep punching at you. But Barry's music is dominated by strings. It's women's music. A lot of violins contrasted by his deep baritone. He floats on top of those strings. Both of 'em are great artists, but their only similarity is their deep voices. And Ike, incidentally, can sing circles around Barry.

"So," Eric continued, "Laura challenged me to write a better review or else stop the criticizing. Since we'd just bought Barry's album I got up and listened to it. Then I wrote a review. She typed it up, proofread it and everything and sent it to *Rolling Stone* magazine. Surprisingly, they printed it. And they very seldom accept stuff that isn't written by one of their own staff, especially from new writers." His reviews, he explained, led to short profiles of artists and finally to covering entire tours.

"Laura must have been very proud of you," Charlene said.

"Well, uh, I guess she would've been. But by this time she was dead."

"That's sad, Eric, that she never saw your success. Funny, Yvonne never mentioned her."

"Yvonne didn't know much about her. I didn't spend very much time with my family around then. I had just gotten out of the service and my head wasn't on too straight. I kept them outta my life for a few months."

Yvonne noticed that Eric's face seemed tortured. She felt

tremendous sympathy for him at that moment. For the first time he appeared vulnerable. There were plenty of questions she wanted to ask him, but didn't want to augment the obvious pain he was experiencing.

"Come on, man." Charlie jumped from the blanket and pulled Eric's arm.

"Come on where?" he protested.

"In the water. Or are you scared?" she asked.

"I ain't scared of nothing!"

"I'll race you to the buoy in the middle and back," she challenged.

"You're on!"

In contrast to Isaac Payne's humble Boston dwelling, the aged and venerable Dr. Michael Solomon occupied a stately mansion in Inglewood, California. Visitors were invariably awestruck at Dr. Solomon's immense estate.

Dr. Solomon sat at the long dining table and looked menacingly at the diners who sat at his table. Jacob Robb toyed with a piece of steak and Joseph Malcolm poured black coffee for himself. "I don't like anything integrated," he was fond of saying, "not even my coffee."

Isaac Payne glanced at a massive chandelier dangling above Solomon's head from the high ceiling and fantasized it crashing down upon his host's head. He dismissed the thought and chided himself for such thinking. Dr. Solomon was, after all, his Muslim brother, fellow scientist and . . . friend? It was hard to think of Mikal Sulaiman as anybody's friend. At eighty, he remained quick witted, imposing and, at 6'4", intimidating. He still seemed vigorous and virile. He'd outlived two wives and was now working on a third, a forty-seven-year-old ex-gymnast.

Though Jacob Robb had a Ph.D. in economics and Joseph Malcolm had one in psychology, only Solomon used the title "doctor" as an inseparable part of his name.

Bernard, Solomon's butler, entered the spacious dining room.

"Will that be all, Doctor?" Bernard spoke with a British accent. Even after all these years Isaac had still not grown accustomed to hearing a black man speak in that manner. He coughed to stifle a chuckle. Isaac knew that Bernard was from Macon, Georgia.

"Yes, thank you, Bernard," replied Dr. Solomon. "I'd like to discuss some things privately now with my guests."

"Very well, sir," Bernard said and walked smartly from the room.

Isaac bit his tongue to keep from laughing out loud.

Mikal, knowing Isaac's "grassroots" lifestyle, wasn't fooled. He knew Isaac found his luxuriant living humorous. He glared at Ishaq.

Mikal had long ago tired of trying to persuade Ishaq to abandon a life of seeming poverty. Had not the Saviour himself promised them money, good homes and friendship in all walks of life? He could not understand a man denying himself these divinely promised pleasures when he could afford them. Isaac was rich. All of them were rich. Allah had so blessed them. They were wrong to deny the favors of Allah.

"Shall we get down to business?" It was more an announcement than a question. "I propose that we continue this in the conference room."

Wordlessly they rose from their seats and filed down the corridor to the conference room. Solomon sometimes referred to it as "the strategy room."

"Ishaq," Solomon addressed Isaac by his Arabic name, "what has been accomplished since last we met?"

"During the past month, Doctor, I located three potential assassins, or operators, if you will. One of them is a woman.

80

Because of the nature of the Messenger's security I had to restrict my choices to blacks, and these had to be American born to speak English fluently and in the Afro-American dialect.''

"Why is that?" asked Solomon.

"Because owing to the nature of the Messenger's security arrangements and the fact that he almost never leaves home these days, the assignment may require that the person infiltrate the Nation of Islam. He may have to find a way into the Messenger's home. To accomplish this the operator will have to be black. White people, as we all know, are not admitted into the Nation of Islam.

"Yes, yes, we know this," said Solomon grumpily.

"Well, there were very few active professionals who met those qualifications," said Isaac.

"You mean to tell me," said Solomon, "that on the whole planet earth there are just a handful of people who are capable of eliminating an old man?"

"They not only have to be black," answered Isaac, "but they have to be American black. Even Africans are denied membership in the Nation. West Indians can get in, but because of their accent they'd attract attention and that we can't have." Isaac allowed them to ponder this momentarily. "This project will require the most professional of methods, immeasurable cunning and almost suicidal daring."

Isaac stopped to look at the doctor. His eyes said that he was trying to be polite, but that he was tired from the flight to the Coast. He'd spent an enormous amount of time choosing the right person and he wasn't up to dealing with Mikal's attitude.

"Please go on, Ishaq." This from Joseph Malcolm. "Obviously you've done quite a bit of work on this project. We're anxious to hear about it."

"To make a long story short, I chose one who . . ."

"What!" Solomon nearly leaped from his chair. "Who authorized you to select an operator without consulting the rest of us?"

"Goddamn it, Mikal. I'm getting fed up with your imperial attitude. This committee is run by four people. Four *equals*. So you can come down off your high and mighty horse. *As you well know,* whomever is charged with implementing a project has *full* control over all technical matters pertaining to it. All the full committee does is determine the overall objective. How it's brought about and by whom is the sole responsibility of the project executive. In this case, that's me. And I didn't want this to begin with. You all selected me. Your jobs are to receive full reports and to offer advice and provide the monies required for the project's success. So, Michael, you can cut out that bullshit because I'm sick of it."

The other men were stunned. While it was true that Solomon wasn't the official head of the committee, he was generally regarded as such and prior to this he'd always been treated accordingly.

"Here! Here!" interrupted Solomon. "Ishaq's right. I was not being fair. Please continue, Ishaq."

If possible, the other members were more astonished than before. It was not often that Mikal Sulaiman apologized for anything.

"The man I selected is Eric Schofield," announced Isaac.

"Eric Schofield?" Joseph Malcolm was puzzled. "I'm sure I've heard that name somewhere before."

"He's a writer," answered Isaac. "He's been getting a lot of publicity lately."

"Ishaq, I realize you know what you're doing. But I find the selection of a writer for this project highly unusual," commented Jacob.

"The writing is a cover. Let me explain. Schofield was

an Army demolitions expert in Vietnam. He had an uncanny aptitude for languages and was a natural for espionage work. He became an all-around 'special operations' man. You know what that includes: defections, assassinations, code breaking, infiltrating the Saigon underworld and using it where advantageous to U.S. interests.''

Isaac saw that his small audience was clinging to his every word. He went on.

''Schofield was suddenly yanked out of Viet Nam and sent to Angola which was becoming a hot bed with MPLA and UNITA both fighting to overthrow the Portuguese. Ironically, they were having skirmishes with each other. Using two separate identities Schofield infiltrated first MPLA and then UNITA. It was his assessment that victory for the guerrillas was a foregone conclusion. The only question was whom it was wisest for America to support. UNITA, he felt, had greater popular support, especially in the South. But MPLA, because of their Cuba-Moscow connection, was better equipped. He advised America to back UNITA and to push for a rapid Portuguese withdrawal.

''He returned to the States in early 1970, disgusted with the military. Rumor has it that while in Africa he learned the U.S. was advising Rhodesian military people to use Klan-style terrorist tactics on their black population. I hardly think anyone would have to advise the Rhodesians to do something they'd already been doing quite well for decades. So I don't put much stock in that. Another rumor says he had to assassinate a high-ranking MPLA member who'd become a close friend of his. I don't know if this rumor is true either. But I do know that Pisces will kill a black as quickly as he will a white. He has shown little concern for racial issues, in a political sense. He loves black music, but that's a natural reaction to his cultural upbringing, not a form of protest or black identity thing.''

"Pisces? What's that?" asked Joseph Malcolm.

"That's his code name. He was born March 10th which makes his astrological sign Pisces, the fish."

"Very interesting," Malcolm said.

"He bummed around for about half a year. Then he started writing. He didn't make any money to speak of until about a year later. In the meantime he scuffled to make ends meet."

"So how'd he get back into the assassination business, for myself I mean?" Jacob asked.

"I'm getting to that. Schofield was living with a girl, one Laura Carlton. They planned to marry once his career, journalism, picked up. Just when things were beginning to turn, Laura became pregnant. Though she fiercely wanted a baby, she reasoned that a child would be too much of a strain on Schofield and that under pressure of supporting a child he'd drop his budding career and get a common job. So Laura sneaked off to have an illegal abortion. Two days after the abortion, Laura began hemorrhaging. Eric, right in bed with her, could do nothing to stop the flow of blood. She died in his arms."

"My!" Dr. Solomon uttered his first sound since clashing with Isaac Payne earlier.

"It turned out that Laura kept a diary and had written down all the information about her pregnancy, their lack of money, and her fears for Schofield's career. Her last entry stated, and I quote, 'The abortion was a success. Oh, I feel so terrible. It was a boy! A little boy who would've been just like my Ricky. I wanted that baby so badly. But Ricky deserves a chance and I'm determined that he get it. Oh, God, please forgive me. Oh Ricky, I wish I could talk to you, tell you about it. I feel lower than dirt.' Eric discovered her diary.

"After getting over the shock he vowed never to be without money again. In his mind it was poverty that killed Laura. And since money runs the world, he was determined to do whatever was required to get his fair share. 'Believe that! I'll get my fair share and more!' were the words he spoke to a friend in a bar not long after Laura's death.

"So Schofield decided to use his already formidable skills to make a large sum of money. He decided to become a mercenary. He even travelled to Africa under an assumed name. But he was soon persuaded to become a professional assassin.

"He re-established some old contacts he'd made while in Army intelligence. He was also able to make some new ones. He has five middlemen, most assassins work through just one, mind you, who arrange contracts in the major centers of the world: Lisbon, Zurich, Cairo, Nairobi and Beirut. He prefers to work outside of the States, but he has occasionally accepted contracts here."

"How'd you get him to take our contract, then?"

"You might say that I made him an offer that he couldn't refuse."

For the first time the men laughed. The laughter was refreshing. They'd been discussing weighty subjects, and they needed a bit of levity.

"Okay, Ishaq," smiled Dr. Solomon. "What's the cost?"

"A quarter of a million dollars."

Simultaneously, the men let out a prolonged "whew!"

"Listen," began Payne, "Schofield is no fool. He knows that he could lose his life on this one. And he also knows that the Muslims will be hunting him down for the remainder of his life. The only job that would cost more would be a hit on a president of a major country. A quarter of a million was par for the course, perhaps a little cheap, all things considered."

"We'll trust your judgment, Ishaq." Dr. Solomon had spoken. "I believe it's customary to pay one half in advance and half upon execution of the contract, am I correct?"

"Yes."

"Then I suggest," continued Dr. Solomon, "that we decide now if we're willing to pay this kind of money. Anyone opposed?"

No one moved or raised a hand.

"Very well then, it's settled," stated Dr. Solomon. "How shall we get the money to him?"

"He has an account in the Cayman Islands," replied Payne. "I have the number. We are to transfer funds to that account within a week if we intend to employ his services."

"What about his middlemen?" asked Jacob Robb. "Don't we have to deal through one of them?"

"Not this time. I bypassed them. I spoke to Schofield directly. The fewer people involved the greater our chances of maintaining secrecy."

Chapter Seven

July, 1974

En route to Tracey's apartment, Eric, in New York again, stopped at several points to make telephone calls. He placed a call to Zurich. No, he wouldn't be available for several months. Another call went to Lisbon. He had no intentions of visiting the country. He'd be in touch when he was free to visit Portugal. That would be several months at the earliest. He called Cairo. Yes, he'd seen the ad in the *New York Times* classified section and knew he was being summoned. No, he was not interested in *"seeing the pyramids"* any time soon.

From his phone calls he learned via the codes they utilized that there were requests for his services in France—"Pierre was wondering when you'd get around to writing him." From South Africa—"I've been thinking of getting her diamonds for our anniversary. What do you think?" And from Egypt—"Wouldn't you like to see the pyramids? Things will be in such an uproar, so upside down, what with the tourists in another month."

The last amused Schofield. To the Egyptian eye, the Star of David featured an upside down pyramid. The mentioning of the pyramids with the term "upside down" was his agent's way of letting Eric know he had a contract, either within Israel or on an Israeli citizen.

During each call Eric had said, "I'm having a terrible time locating Mary. Have you heard from her?" Cairo, Zurich, Lebanon, Nairobi and Lisbon all answered that they hadn't heard a word from her.

"Mary" was America. Which meant that no American had inquired into purchasing Schofield's service. Nor were any of the contracts which were being sought to be carried out on American soil.

So who is the old man working for? Who is it that wants Elijah Muhammad assassinated, he wondered. Schofield sought to know as much as he could about his employer. Too often clients got after-the-fact jitters and tried to cover their tracks by eliminating their employees. Schofield had no intention of being caught unawares, if he could help it. So he endeavored to know his sponsors and also the hired hands who did their dirty work but were incapable of carrying out or setting up a complex assassination.

Who was it who wanted Elijah dead? He hoped to find out. But he'd already agreed to carry out the contract for the two hundred fifty thousand dollars.

He would begin his research even without having his employer's actual identity. But in the course of his activities he intended to learn just who the contract's sponsor was.

His last call was to the Cayman Islands. The bank president informed him that, yes, there had been a deposit made to his account. His new balance reflected a $125,000 increase.

88

It was now official. Elijah Muhammad would die.

"Can I get you a drink?" asked Tracey.

"Thanks. Bacardi and Coke."

Schofield didn't know how Tracey would react to the news he was about to tell her. Their relationship was a little weird, he thought. Weird in that he could not easily define it. Its buddy-buddy quality had continued despite their lovemaking which had begun months ago. But there was an added dimension to their relationship and he didn't know the ground rules. But, while he didn't want to hurt her, he hoped she wasn't counting on tying him down. He didn't think so. She seemed to cherish her freedom too.

Maybe he didn't need a label placed on their relationship. Maybe labels were too inhibiting, too stifling to facilitate natural emotional growth. Though he was hard put to fully understand what he actually felt for Tracey, he did know that he cared for her deeply, but as a sweet and invigorating human being who also happened to turn him on sexually. He felt something romantic, that was certain. He always looked forward to seeing her. Yet he never ached to be with her when he was away. No, it was never like that; never like it was when he was away from Laura.

Tracey returned with two glasses of rum and Coke. Eric hadn't noticed that he was seated in the loveseat until Tracey settled in beside him.

"I think they're going to make a movie out of it," she said after several silent seconds.

"Huh?"

"The book. There's talk of a movie."

"No shit!" Eric was surprised. Sure, he hoped that maybe Hollywood would pick up his novel, nearly all writers did. But he was astonished at the rapidity of the progress.

He asked, "Have negotiations already started?"

"Started yesterday. I'll bring you in when we've gotten close to a basic agreement," said Tracey.

"If that's gonna be anytime in the next six months, don't bother," he said. "I'll just have to trust your judgment like I always do."

"And what's going to prevent you from getting involved during the next six months?" She was steeling herself for another of Schofield's personality peculiarities.

"I'm going away for a while," answered Schofield.

"Going away?" For a second a wave of disappointment traversed her face. But she recovered swiftly. "Where?"

"A few places in Europe. I just feel like taking some time off to do a little traveling. Not for business, but for pleasure. I can finally afford it, and I don't want to put it off any longer. It's something I've been wanting to do for the longest time. This'll be one of the few times I've been abroad for myself, not for the Army."

Then they discussed the movie. Tracey had to strain to keep her mind on the conversation instead of Eric's imminent departure. Eric assured her again that he had the utmost confidence in her ability to obtain the best possible deal. No, he couldn't get involved with the screenplay and he didn't want to get credit for the work a "ghost" might do.

Eric knew that there were studios that liked to list the author of a novel adapted to the screen as the screenwriter. This gave the movie an aura of authenticity. Eric didn't want credit for anybody else's work and he didn't want to be criticized for their blunders either.

"Eric, are you sure you're not sneaking away to research a new book?" asked Tracey accusingly.

"Course not. I just want some freedom for a while, a chance to lay back, you know."

"If you are planning to write a new book, Eric, I should know."

"Tracey, I haven't even decided *if* I'm ever gonna write another book, let alone be prepared to research it. If I do decide to write again, you'll know about it before the ink dries on paragraph one."

Tracey studied him to see if there was any significance to his implication that he might give up writing. Eric was so strange, so unpredictable, she decided that there was no way for her to tell. She would just let it hang there where it was. There were other things, more immediately important, that needed to be discussed. And with Eric planning his European trip, she knew she had to accelerate the pace she'd planned.

"You know, we haven't talked in a long time, Eric."

Her eyes seemed to sparkle, almost as if there were tears collecting in them. Yet they were very dry, bright and alert. He'd never paid a lot of attention to her eyes before.

His eyes drew in the image of the smooth brown skin which clothed her high cheekbones, giving her an oriental cast. Today there seemed to be a slight reddishness to her skin tone.

"Things have been happening so fast, there hasn't been time," Eric said.

Eric felt not a little embarrassed. But this was their first night alone in a long time and he felt a little awkward.

"As well as I know you, sometimes I feel like I don't really know you at all. Behind all your kidding and joking there's something hidden and mysterious. Perhaps even dangerous."

Tracey was trying to tell him something, he knew her well enough to know that. But she was approaching whatever it was with extreme caution.

"Go on," Eric said.

"You remember my boyfriend Nathan?" He did. She'd spoken of him many times. "Well, we broke up because I wouldn't give up my work to marry him. Okay, it hurt, but

91

I made that choice. I'm dedicated to my work. I want to be something or somebody or whatever.''

"Got you covered," he said, "go on."

"I care a lot for you. In a way I love you. But I'm not ready for anything too heavy. I love you as a person. I'm attracted to you physically as a man. But I can't let anything interfere with my career. So, I don't want to mislead you or use you. I like being with you and I'm no iron maiden. I need a man sometimes. I'm glad that that man is you. But I wanted this on the table so that nobody would get hurt or anything. If you have problems with that, let me know and we'll cut off the romance.''

Eric almost laughed. She looked so pitiful when she spoke. She seemed like a person who had just confessed to murder. He stifled the laugh that was building in his stomach, knowing that this wasn't a time for humor. She was serious and what she'd said hadn't been easy for her to say.

"Tracey, what you're saying is perfectly candid and mature. Under the circumstances I think this is best. Both of us have other priorities. I like being with you too. But I was worried about our thing getting so deep that it obstructed progress in other areas.''

"Well, I'm glad that's out of the way," she said. "Now come over here and give me a kiss.''

"Gladly," he said.

She poured two more drinks.

"To sanity and maturity," she toasted.

They spoke about the book, things in general, some of her other clients, and when they noticed the time, it was well past midnight.

They talked of some of their past relationships. She told him about Nathan, about her pain over their separation, and how she'd often wondered if she could ever give herself totally to a man.

He spoke of Laura, of his fear of becoming wrapped up in a woman again.

That night he slept with her. He awakened before she did. He pushed back the hair that was covering the right side of her face. Then he kissed her face. She looked adorable in her sleep. His kisses trailed down her neck and her small bosom.

Now she was awake. She moaned over the warm kisses he pasted on her chest. She reached up to caress his face, moved her hands over his shoulders. Then, with surprising strength for so small a woman, she pulled him toward her.

He was sorry that he had to go to "Europe" at all.

Chapter Eight

The collection officer was surprised when Eric Schofield informed him that he wanted to pay his rent for six more months in advance. His rent was already paid for three advance months, so this payment seemed unusual.

Schofield explained that he planned to travel to Europe and might be away for several months. This seemed to satisfy the representative's curiosity and, knowing that Eric was a writer, he assumed that he was either researching a book or touring with one of those insufferable rock groups. He'd probably find his daughter reading the article in one of those godless hippie magazines.

That taken care of, Eric packed the items he'd need. His habit was to travel light. He neither wanted to be encumbered by a bulk of material he didn't really need nor to possibly leave a trace of his presence.

That afternoon he drove to Philadelphia. He wanted to

obtain as much information as possible about Elijah Muhammad. He knew of a Muslim-owned newsstand at 52nd and Market streets that displayed several books by Muhammad.

Months previously, a girl he'd taken out told him to drive up Market Street so she could get a bean pie.

"A bean pie?" he'd questioned incredulously.

"Yeah, a bean pie. You've never had one? They're delicious."

"A bean pie. Damn. How can you eat something like that?"

When he'd come to 52nd Street Eric dashed over to the newsstand. He purchased two pies. He then noticed several Muslim publications and assumed this was one of the many Muslim businesses that were springing up all over Philadelphia.

"I must confess this bean pie is outta sight," Eric had said when he'd tasted it.

Now Eric would return to the same stand to begin research on the man he had agreed to kill.

"Excuse me," Eric said to the clean-shaven Muslim who operated the stand. "I'm trying to locate some books by Elijah Muhammad."

"You came to the right place, brother. We got *Message to the Blackman, How to Eat to Live, The Fall of America,* and *Our Saviour Has Arrived* by the Most Honorable Elijah Muhammad. We also have a book by Brother Minister Bernard Cushmeer, *This Is The One.* It's about the Messenger."

"I'd like one copy of each."

"All right. How about a copy of *Muhammad Speaks?*" the Muslim asked.

Eric gave him twenty-five cents for the tabloid newspaper.

"I'm trying to get some other books. Books about Elijah,

uh, Muhammad. I mean, I'm looking for things written by other people. You know, non-Muslims.''

"Why you looking for that kinda stuff, brother, when right in your hands are the words of the Messenger himself? Would you rather find out about a man from somebody else or would you rather go to the man directly?'' asked the young Muslim. "Hey! Check it out. Who can tell you better than the man himself? You don't need that other junk. It's poison, man. Most of that stuff is one hundred percent poison.''

It was obvious to Eric that he was dealing with a man whose eyes had seen the glory of the coming of the Lord. Such eyes, he thought, might locate the Lord with no trouble. But the same eyes would be unable to see dogshit waiting expectantly on the pavement for the owner's feet.

He tried another approach.

"I need the books for school. I'm a teacher. Social studies. And my class, when school starts, will spend several weeks on the Black Muslims. So, you know how whitey is. He wants me to be 'objective.' Meaning I have to include some of the books *he* approves. It's jive, but I gotta go along with it if I want my students to learn the truth from Elijah, the Messenger, I mean.''

"Hey! I didn't know you was getting this for school.'' The Muslim was now less defensive. "What school you teach at?''

"Uh, Edison. Edison High.''

"Hey man! My little brother goes there. Might be in your class. Name's Tyrone Dennis.''

"Well, I'll keep an eye out for him. So where do you think I could get some other books on the Messenger?'' asked Eric.

"You might try Hakim's on 52nd and Walnut, right down the street. Then there's Robin's on 13th right off Market. Out in Germantown you might check Uhuru Kitabu. They should have the books you're looking for.''

"Thanks, brother. I'll check them out. Take it easy now."
"Yes sir! As-Salaam-Alaikum."
"Yeah. Right."

Chapter Nine

Two weeks later Schofield had rented a house at 3800 Mellon Street in West Philadelphia. The rent was cheap and, he found, better for his needs than an apartment would be because he didn't have to worry as much about nosey neighbors concerning themselves with his coming and going or his hours. He needed as much anonymity as he could find for research on his subject. He was glad to be free of the hotel that he'd stayed in until locating the house.

Whenever possible, while on assignment, Eric preferred staying in a house over staying in an apartment. This house had come furnished, and that was another plus. Also, it was a corner house so only one side was close to another building. If he could only get used to the driving music that rushed through his windows from the speakeasy bar across the street he'd be all right.

Schofield sat at the kitchen table and surrounded himself

with numerous books on Elijah Muhammad and the Nation of Islam. Several editions of *Muhammad Speaks* were also there.

Soon he knew as much about the movement as most of the church's ministers. But there was still a whole lot of the Messenger's articles he hadn't read that might contain something pertinent to his mission. He'd found out that Elijah had, prior to starting *Muhammad Speaks,* written articles in *The Pittsburgh Courier, The Amsterdam News* and *The Los Angeles Herald-Dispatch.* He wasn't sure if he'd be able to track down all of these pieces, but he would definitely have to read some of those old editions of *Muhammad Speaks.*

Tomorrow he'd go to the University of Pennsylvania library to check out some of the Messenger's old writings. The Penn library had all of the *Muhammad Speaks* editions on microfilm.

Schofield's eyes had read as much Muslim theology as they could take for one day. He'd skimmed through several editions of *Muhammad Speaks* and figured he'd had enough of Elijah's philosophy for one day. The pieces that he'd found particularly interesting he'd photocopied for later study.

He'd decided that he had learned more about the Muslim personality from reading *The Autobiography of Malcolm X,* C. Eric Lincoln's *Black Muslims in America* and E. U. Essien-Udom's *Black Nationalism* than he had from Elijah's own writings.

Elijah's work was mainly religious stuff mixed with exhortations for the black man to "get up and do something for self."

Eric got up, not to do something for self, but to get out of the library. His back bumped into something. That something was soft and not at all unpleasant.

"Oh," a startled female voice exclaimed.

"Sorry," Eric said, slightly embarrassed. "I didn't know

you were behind me."

"It's my fault. Just surprised me, your getting up so abruptly. I was going to ask you if you'd mind showing me how to work the microfilm machine. I'm new to this."

Eric sized her up. High yellow complexion, jet black hair that draped over her shoulders. Midi-skirt that failed to obscure well-shaped calves from his view. She stood about five feet six, appeared to be in her early twenties and her face was an agreeable cross between sharp and rounded features. Her eyes were dark ovals that hid behind incredibly long lashes. He looked down at her cutout shoes and took a peek at her feet. More than anything Schofield was turned off by ugly feet. What he beheld did not succeed in turning him off. On the contrary, he was impressed. Her strong toes looked out of the openings revealing well-manicured nails. She had high arches, thick ankles and small heels.

He tore his eyes away from her dogs and travelled due north, past her tapered waist to her breasts that, deprived of bra, pushed through her blouse at him.

Here was true beauty. Yet there seemed to be a reticence about her, an unwillingness to fully accent or flaunt her beauty. Then Eric noticed that she wore no makeup.

On a purely physical level, Schofield was devastated.

"Um, sure. Be glad to show you how to work these bad boys," he said, pointing at the machines.

"I hope I'm not taking you away..."

"Oh no. Don't you worry 'bout a thing. I was finished anyway."

"Well, if you're sure. I really would appreciate it."

They picked out a microfilm projector and she sat at it. Looking up at him she said, "My name's Marsha. Yours?"

"Kevin," replied Eric. "Kevin Stone."

She extended a slender, well-manicured hand.

"Pleased to meet you, Kevin."

Schofield proceeded to place the microfilm into the machine while explaining the technique.

"I don't mean to be newsy,"—in Eric's hometown "nosey" was pronounced "newsy"—"but what are you looking for?"

"There was an article in the *New York Times* in November of 1970 about genetic engineering. I don't know if you're familiar with the subject. I don't have the exact date, so I've got to go through everything in that month."

"Wow! That's tedious work. Tell you what. I'm finished with what I was doing. I'll help you find the article. I'll take half the month and you take the other half. Together we should cut the time in half."

"Oh no," said Marsha. "I could never impose . . ."

"Forget it. No imposition. And after we find it you can tell me a little bit about genetic engineering. Deal?"

Her expression said that she saw Eric's motives. They were advertised in his eyes. She appeared to consider it, then the corners of her mouth curved upwards in a smile.

"A deal," she said.

They fed spools of microfilm to the machine. The machine devoured them, giving back a picture of every page of the *Times*.

It was a monstrous job that, a half hour later, was still only partially done.

Schofield realized that he'd been so mesmerized by Marsha's beauty that he'd forgotten to utilize the reference books which tell you precisely which page and which date a particular article is on.

"Hey, did you check out the reference index for the *Times*? That'll tell us exactly where we can find the piece."

"I asked for it, but the librarian said someone had lifted the book, and they'd ordered another that has yet to come in."

"Bullshit," said Schofield.

Eric walked to the young man's desk.

"Look here, buddy. We're trying to find an article on genes. Not blue jeans, genetic genes. Now, it's in a November issue of *The New York Times* and I'd appreciate it if you'd check that little book of yours and let me know the date of publication and the page it's located on."

"Very sorry, sir. But the edition provided for public use has, ah, disappeared."

"Look, punk. You think I'm a damn fool? I've been here for over three hours and I don't feel like playing games. I want the date. I know damned well you keep a copy for employee use. Now go find that date before I have to put my foot up your ass."

Eric hoped he came off like he was so mad he was just barely in control. When the young guy's eyes widened in shock and fear Eric struggled to keep from laughing. He didn't even know if they had an extra copy, but he was gambling that they did.

Involuntarily the young man's hand covered his buttocks. He stood frozen, looking at Schofield with a mixture of astonishment and fear. He didn't often encounter angry niggers. When he overcame his surprise he turned away, hand still pasted to his ass, and entered a small office. Moments later he returned with the book.

Eric leafed through it, found what he wanted, and returned it to the frightened young librarian.

"Thanks, sweetie," chimed Eric, pleased over his prank.

When he returned to Marsha she said, "I don't find your little performance cute in the least. You nearly scared that boy to death. I heard every word you said and it was horrible."

"Time out, momma!" Eric said, his eyes tightening in anger. "I was just trying to find something *you* needed. You

102

should be hot with him, not me. He's the one that lied to you, told you he didn't have the book. So if you wanna take up for that lying little fairy, go ahead.''

He thrust a sheet of paper at her. "Here's the date. Me? I'll catch you later. *Much* later.''

He picked up his papers and books and hurried to the door.

"Kevin! Wait a minute!''

Schofield stopped. He didn't really want to split anyway. She walked to him.

"I'm sorry. You're right. I had no right to come down on you like that. Please forgive me.''

She looked like a doe, a reindeer, with her eyes wide with contrition and hope.

"Besides,'' she smiled mischievously, "I haven't fulfilled *my* part of our agreement yet.''

Her smile widened and Eric was treated to a keyboard of shining white teeth.

Schofield had intended to play hard-to-pacify, but he found himself grinning like the proverbial Cheshire cat. What the fuck, he thought. If you're gonna be weak it might as well be for women.

She copied the *Times* article and put it in her folder. They left the library.

Eric's car, a used Pinto he'd recently bought, was parked on Walnut Street. They drove downtown to a restaurant in center city called Fast Eddies. Over soft music and wine they got to know something about each other.

Eric looked at Marsha through the soft reflection of multi-hued lights.

"So you advocate cloning,'' he said, somewhat amused.

"Certainly. When people get over their superstitions and their silly pseudo-theological oppositions to everything scientific, they'll see that genetic engineering holds great promise for the human race in the future.'' She sipped more wine. "Look, Kevin," she continued, "whenever science comes up with something progressive people complain that it's the work of the devil. If science listened to the common people, who do no more than echo their ignorant ministers, on things related to science we'd never have escaped the dark ages. There'd be no air travel, no telephones, no ovens, no modern medicine. People would still be dying from smallpox and children would still be misshapen from polio, those who didn't die outright."

"Yeah, but this thing is tampering with nature. Gives me the creeps," said Eric.

"Well, I think 'nature's way' is for Man to control his life and destiny, as far as he is able. I know that with cloning we can feed starving people, we can produce transplants that the body won't reject because the organ will be the same as the original one. Identical! Exact number of cells. The only difference is that it'll be healthy. A lot of people can't get a heart or kidney transplant. People aren't exactly standing in line waiting to donate their hearts and kidneys, you know."

They both laughed.

"I just feel cloning people is weird," opined Eric.

"Frankly, I don't think that's even necessary. In the future, science will be able to stimulate the growth of a single organ. So we won't be creating whole people. Not a whole body, just a heart or whatever organ is needed."

"So people will be going to the supermarket to pick up a couple of lungs after they burn theirs out with cigarettes and smog. Purchase a new eyeball or two, maybe a new brain eventually. I know a lot of niggers that can use new brains."

Marsha laughed politely. She didn't particularly like jokes that tended to degrade black people.

"This is too heavy for me. Tell me, Marsha, how is this done? I mean, what exactly do they do to clone something?"

"There are a couple of methods. But the two major techniques currently under experimentation involve the removal of the cell's nucleus either chemically or by incision. Now, let's just say we were going to clone a man. We'd take a body cell. Not a gamete. Never a reproductive cell. But, say, a kidney cell. They're very good. Theoretically, we could even use a hair cell or a bone cell. The DNA, deoxyribonucleic acid, instructions are written in every cell. So we'd cut the nucleus out of the outlining protoplasm. Then we'd take a female ovum and remove its nucleus. With me so far?"

"Just barely," said Eric. "Go on."

"When the cell nucleus is placed within the protoplasm of the female gamete, the cell reacts like it would if it had been fertilized in the conventional manner. After it's implanted into a female womb it begins to divide. Mitosis or cell multiplication takes place. Eventually the man, the donor, is fully reproduced. The new organism has all of the physical attributes of the donor and none of the female who provided the ovum."

"Why is that?" asked Eric. "How come the donor is fully reproduced and not the mother?"

"Because," Marsha answered pedantically, "the female nucleus, where her DNA are, was removed. See, a person is born with twenty-three chromosomes from the female and twenty-three from the male. The body cells, reflecting this equal contribution from mom and dad, have forty-six chromosomes. But the sex cells only have half the required forty-six. The chromosomes contain the DNA instructions which are the virtual blueprint which determines the body's most minute characteristics.

"The female reproductive cell is designed to begin reproducing once it is complete with the twenty-three chromosomes from the male sperm cell. When the body cell nucleus—which already has the full forty-six chromosomes—is placed inside the ovum protoplasm, it 'thinks' it's been fertilized and begins the job of reproduction accordingly. And that's why the new life has none of the female's looks but all of the donor's. Because all of the chromosomes came from the donor who, in this case, is a male."

Eric said: "And this kind of stuff is going on? You people are experimenting with this?"

"Not me, not yet. I'm still in the theoretical stage. Just a med student. But I hope to do research in recombinant DNA in the near future."

"You ready to split? I think I've had a sufficient dosage of Fast Eddies famed atmosphere."

She was ready. Eric picked up the check. They walked to the lot where the Pinto was parked.

"Where to, Mademoiselle?" asked Eric after they'd gotten in the car.

She shared an apartment on Spruce Street not far from the University of Pennsylvania hospital. Her roommate, a law student, was with her parents in Nebraska. So Marsha had the place to herself for the summer.

Eric pulled up in front of her building. She paused for a moment, seemingly undecided.

"It's been a very pleasant evening, Marsha." He waited until she'd entered the building before he drove off.

Over the next two weeks he took her out often. They went to ballgames, attended concerts, and saw movies whenever Schofield's schedule permitted it. In the meantime he read the literature he had on Elijah Muhammad and attended as many meetings as he could at the Muslim Temple on 13th and Susquehanna Avenue.

One night, after a dinner date, Marsha asked if Eric would like to come up for a minute. She blushed when she asked, an ashamed look on her face.

"Does a bear shit in the woods?" Eric responded.

She laughed. She usually detested profanity and vulgarity. But from him it sounded almost cute. He was an unusual one. He seemed to shift almost constantly from suburbanite to street nigger and back again. But neither identity seemed affected. He wore both naturally and, she noted, quite well.

"Come on, then," she said.

Marsha showed him around the small apartment. He saw that although the inhabitants were going through the expected collegiate ritual of living sparsely, obvious signs of affluence were there.

The furniture was not cheap and gaudy, but of high quality and selected with the confidence of a person who had no need to display wealth. The stereo set was of especially high quality, but it was obviously not new. Someone had brought it from home with them, which suggested parents who purchased their children the best. Those traits would naturally be instilled in the offspring as surely as hair texture or height.

The apartment had only a single bedroom, but Eric was pleased to see two beds. A lot of young women thought nothing of sharing a bed, but Eric had always thought there was something weird in that. He couldn't see himself even sharing a room with a dude, much less a bed. That was one of the things he liked about the assignments he had in the Army. Very little contact was required with the other men. He usually worked alone. Apart from basic training and periods of transition for re-assignment, he spent little time in the barracks with the other men. In fact, he didn't really enjoy the company of other men that much. He had no close male friends. His free time was either spent in the company of females or alone.

Eric had a theory that if you wanted to know where a chick was at mentally you checked out her record collection, her wall paintings or posters and her library. When two or more lived together it was harder to make an assessment. But eventually you got to the point where you could decide which record belonged to whom and what painting was the property of whom.

Marsha had a bookcase made of polished wood boards and cinderblocks. It was delightfully incongruent with the rest of the apartment.

"We made it ourselves," Marsha said as she watched Eric studying the case. "We even carried all the bricks up ourselves," she added proudly. "We stole them," a giggle, "from a construction site." Now her chin jutted out in defiance. "Shoot! They tore down a health clinic to build a damn office building. Serves them right." Now a bit shyly, "You don't think they'll miss them, do you? I mean, the cost wasn't all that much."

The bookcase stretched almost to the ceiling. The upper portion was filled with science, biology and medical texts. There were also a large number of books by Isaac Asimov: *The Human Body*, *The Human Brain*, *The Genetic Code*, *Wellsprings of Life* and others.

"You're big on Asimov, aren't you?" asked Eric. "I just read his science fiction now and then. Can't handle the hard stuff."

"He writes on scientific subjects for laymen," said Marsha. "I like to read his work to refresh my memory on things. Some of the other books are so technical that I hate to read them any more than necessary. But when I begin med school it'll be all of that technical stuff like the anatomy of crawfish and things like that."

Eric worked his way over to her albums. Leonard Bernstein? Jesus! Tchaikovsky? Christ! The New York Philharmonic Orchestra? Holy Willie Mays!

"This your shit?" he asked.

Marsha must have thought that quite hilarious. She laughed uproariously.

"Those are Ellen's records. My roommate. She loves classical music."

"If you don't mind my asking, what, ah, race is the dear child?" Eric asked.

"Ellen?" more laughter. "Why, she's black, of course."

"Oh."

"What, you think only white people like classical music?" asked Marsha.

"Let's just say that I have not often come across black people who were enthusiastic over that mode of musical expression," said Eric.

Still flipping albums, he came upon an Eddie Kendricks album, two by Roberta Flack, the Chi-Lites, the Jackson 5, the Intruders and one by Donny Hathaway.

"A friend of mine had a party last week and I left most of my records over there. You want to hear some music?" Marsha asked.

"You pick out something," Eric said.

She selected an album from the back of the stack. "This is something I like by Amosisi Leontopolis Thomas—Leon Thomas."

The album was called *Spirits Unknown*.

She put the album on and, bringing the album jacket with her, sat down next to Schofield. The record playing was "The Creator Has a Master Plan."

"This is Leon Thomas' first solo album. He's recorded before with Pharoah Sanders," Marsha was saying. "And look, all of the Pharoah's sidemen, Cecil McBee, Lonnie Liston Smith, are on the album with him."

"No shit," Eric said.

"Yes. But look at who's playing saxophone. 'Little Rock.' Who in the world is Little Rock?" she asked rhetorically.

"Beats my pants," said Eric. He was smiling.

"Well, I happen to know that Pharoah Sanders is from Little Rock, Arkansas, and I'm sure that this Little Rock is actually Pharoah. He must have had a contract that didn't allow him to perform on other labels or something. This album is on the Flying Dutchman label. Pharoah records with Impulse. I think it's the same guy, what do you think?"

"Well, cutie pie," began Eric, "you may have something there."

"I get the distinct impression that you aren't into jazz," said Marsha with disappointment in her eyes.

"What makes you say that?" asked Eric.

"Well, I mean you seem, you know, distracted. Like you think jazz is outside your interests."

"I find *you* very distracting," said Eric.

"I don't know how I should take that," replied Marsha.

"Allow me to put it like this. I like jazz very much. It's one of the art forms I find most interesting. And I was already a fan of Pharoah Sanders back when he was doing *Selflessness* with John Coltrane and *Om* and stuff like that with Trane. I played *Tauhid,* his first featured album, till the grooves came off. And, since some of this album by Leon Thomas features a cut from Pharoah's own *Karma* album, I am inclined to agree that 'Little Rock' is probably Pharoah. But I confess. I was struggling to retain a focus on your very informative words because my attention was being constantly distracted." Eric looked at her earnestly.

"Distracted?" Marsha was confused. "By what?"

"My imagination," said Eric.

"Your imagination? I'm afraid I don't understand."

"I kept imagining," Eric said, "what it would be like to make love to you."

"Listen, Kevin, I. . .I don't want you to get the wrong impression. I didn't invite you here because. . .I'm not that

110

kind of...oh shoot.''

Schofield noticed that she had dropped the album cover onto the floor.

"Sorry if I startled you, honey. Didn't mean to. See, I believe in being honest and direct. And I don't believe that a whole bunch of preliminaries and rituals are necessary for people who like each other, who feel the surge of special feeling for each other. All that stuff is unnecessary to me. If they want to get it on, who is to say that they have to bullshit around for a million years before they do so. So I'm a firm believer in going straight to the point. I like you. I'd like to make love to you. And I really think you'd like to, too. What the heck! I might walk outta here and get run over by a trolley or something.''

He stopped to see if his words were having any effect.

"I'll leave my phone number here on the table.'' He wrote seven digits. "If you get over your shock and feel like I feel, call me. You stay sweet now, I'm cutting out.'' Eric stood to leave. Marsha got up too but, instead of heading to the door, she walked to the table, picked up the slip of paper, and then walked to the phone.

At the door Eric stopped to ask, "Who you calling? The men in white jackets?''

"I'm dialing this number you left,'' replied Marsha. "You said if I ever start to feel like you feel, I should...'' She paused, her eyes boring into his, challenging him.

She sure recovers fast, thought Eric. Too fast? Shit. Who gives a damn.

Schofield was in the purgatorial state between sleep and consciousness, rolling in the bliss of sweet exhausting sex, when he felt movement disturbing him, pulling him out of suspended animation.

He opened his eyes and saw that Marsha was up and

111

beginning to dress. Reflexively, he looked at his watch. It was 2:30 A.M. He'd dozed off somewhere around 2:00 A.M. which meant that there'd been more than an hour of adult calisthenics.

Damn! That chick should've been dead to the world. Must be getting out of shape, he thought. He smiled at his own vain thoughts. Every nigger in the world swears he's another Iceberg Slim.

"What's up?" he asked her sleepily.

"Oh. Look who's awake," she said cheerily.

"What you getting dressed for?"

"Go back to sleep. I'm just going out for cigarettes."

He hadn't recalled seeing her smoke.

"At this hour? You'll get mugged."

"Then I'll get the chance to see if my karate lessons are worth the money," she said.

"Your what?"

"Just kidding. Go back to sleep. I'll be back in a moment," she told him.

Eric wasn't into the various ideologies of women's lib versus male chauvinism, etc. His basic philosophy was that, outside of business, if a chump or chick didn't get in his way or block his moves, he didn't get too stretched out over what they did. But he felt guilty laying in bed while a woman got up at 2:30 in the morning to go and hunt for smokes in West Philadelphia. Like, there was a limit to the equality of the sexes, and he felt that he'd be chumping himself off if he didn't do something.

"Hey, babycakes. I got some smokes."

"What kind you smoke, Winstons?" she asked.

"Yeah. Taste good like a cancer stick should. Take these." He reached for his pack.

"Yech," she said. "Can't stand 'em. I smoke Virginia Slims. My contribution to the women's movement."

112

Suddenly Eric's mind was in overdrive. All of a sudden she gotta smoke when I ain't seen her smoke all day. This is some weird shit. Maybe this is a setup. After she leaves, the big boys kick the doors in and there goes Miranda's baby boy. Damn! I'm starting to get too wrapped up in this cloak and dagger shit. But, then, I do it myself, don't I? Maybe somebody's turning the tables on the old boy.

"Go back to bed, Marsha. I'll go."

"No really, Kevin. You don't have to get up. I'm perfectly capable of..."

"Get in the damn bed. Shit. I already gotta go out in the middle of the night. Ain't gotta listen to no backtalk along with it."

She looked at him, confused. He flashed a toothy smile to indicate that he was kidding.

He jumped up from the bed and pulled on his pants, leaving his drawers under the chair where they'd been tossed.

"Throw me my shirt," he said.

Pulling on his shoes, he looked at her lecherously.

"You gonna have to pay for this chivalry of mine," he said.

She blushed. Damn she's fine, he thought. Almost don't care if she is setting me up. Pussy's good as all outdoors.

"You shouldn't write checks you may be unable to cash," she teased.

"Oh, I can cash it, baby. When I finish, you ain't never gonna think about another nigger."

Almost to herself she said softly, "I can't think of any others already."

This chick is fucking with my head. Better watch out. Can't be getting involved emotionally. Can't stand the pressure.

Eric closed the door behind himself and walked down the hall. Marsha heard his feet almost banging on the tiled floor, as if to purposely wake up the sleeping neighbors. From a distance she heard him yell, "Keep it warm for me."

She considered some of his antics foolish, but she did like him. At first she didn't think she would. Actually, she'd never met anyone quite like him. She'd come from a very well-to-do family and had had little contact with grassroots blacks. The men frightened her and she had nothing in common with the women. Yet she always found something lacking in the young men of her own social class. They seemed almost feminine at times. She had noticed how inadequate they seemed, how they seemed to shrink back in the presence of ghetto blacks.

But this one, Kevin Stone, was a rare bird. He was both street hustler and black academician. He appealed to her urge to break from the aristocratic background she'd grown up in, with his raw, earthy language. But he made her feel comfortable and at home when his moods shifted into more cultured areas, when his language became almost scholarly.

Still, she'd committed herself to doing something, so, though she had no idea why, she'd go through with it. It wasn't a very big thing anyway. She reached for the phone.

After dialing the area code and number she heard the familiar voice that she loved so well.

"Grandpa? It's Marsha."

Isaac Payne said, "Hello darling. I was most concerned. I almost called you."

When Schofield left the apartment, the nagging feeling that something was rotten in the cotton continued to trouble him. Too many professionals before him had bitten the dust because of an unprofessional trust in a beautiful woman.

In Vietnam he'd learned to rely upon instinct and intuition. It was his sixth sense that appeared like an angelic spirit during times of duress. Once, near Saigon, he was going to a general's home to have dinner. The South Vietnamese general was trying hard to impress Eric that the Vietnamese people recognized the growing role blacks were playing in U.S. affairs. He'd gone out of his way to be hospitable to the young black American Army intelligence officer.

When Eric reached the general's home, a strong feeling, almost like an electric shock, hit him. He felt it viscerally. Something was wrong. He stealthily crept away from the general's home and called the number, saying he'd had an accident and would not be able to keep the dinner date. He then returned to the vicinity of the general's home and waited. Less than ten minutes later several men stepped rapidly through the general's door and walked in separate directions, disappearing around corners.

Eric knew who they were. Vietcong. Two days later he crept into the general's home and waited until he returned. Eric hid in a small closet. When the general came home his wife prepared a Western style dinner. Eric's stomach cried out for some of the beef liver that the peasants rarely got even a sniff of.

The general's wife left the dining room with the dishes, obviously to tidy up. The general, comfortable and satiated, leaned back and lit a Cuban cigar. Eric had thought of the big shots ninety miles away from Cuba in Florida who couldn't get one of those babies across that small stretch of sea.

The general's chubby baby boy banged away with a spoon on a plate, sitting in his highchair. The baby was perhaps fifteen months old.

Schofield had emerged from the closet and began creeping up behind the general. The baby started giggling, obviously thinking the strange man was playing a game with him. The general stretched and began a yawn. But he never completed it. The wire which Eric carried in both hands was swiftly wrapped around the general's corpulent neck and pulled tightly until trickles of blood oozed through the soft skin.

The general stiffened at contact and tried to pull the wire with his hands, but the more he struggled the deeper the wire cut.

The baby banged away joyously and laughed aloud. With a final yank and twist, blood spurted out over Eric's clothing and the general's head flopped oddly to one side. When the wife called to her husband, Eric grunted in response and softly walked out of the house.

The same instinctive feeling was assaulting his nerves at the moment. Once again intuition was giving him a warning.

After walking loudly down the corridor of Marsha's apartment he crept back up softly and listened silently outside her door. He had hoped against hope that this time his sixth sense had alarmed him needlessly. He hoped she'd undressed and curled back up in bed, waiting for his return.

But, deep within himself, he knew that no such thing would be happening. Because he suddenly remembered that there were no ashtrays in the apartment. He'd had to use a paper cup for an ashtray, and in his sleepy state he'd forgotten. Marsha didn't smoke.

He waited, not knowing whether he should go to his car for his gun in case would-be assassins came up the stairs, or if he should listen to see if she used the telephone.

He didn't have to make up his mind. The sound of the telephone dialing made it up for him. The building was absolutely silent. He heard her dial again. And again. Eleven numbers he counted in all. She was dialing long distance.

Tension burned within his chest. Conflicting emotions assaulted his brain. This lady had moved him as none had since Laura. And now he would have to . . .

"Grandpa," he heard her say and he almost shouted for joy. She wasn't setting him up. She was calling her grandfather. She probably was worried about the old guy, whoever he was, and was checking up on him. If he's on

116

the Coast somewhere, it's probably not yet midnight. Damn! Was he happy! He felt like kissing the door. Shit. Not only would he bring her back cigarettes, but he'd track down some champagne too. Since he knew the after hours joints, he expected no trouble in finding a bottle even at this hour. She'd be surprised and wonder why he was celebrating. Early Christmas. She would be his Christmas present. Not having to kill her would be present enough.

In his euphoria he knelt there on his knees, his face leaning against the door. He was exhausted from the tension he'd felt earlier. He was rising to his feet when he heard her speak.

"No, grandpa, he didn't have a gun. Yes, I'm sure. He just left a couple of minutes ago. Of course I'm all right. No, he suspects nothing. He's using the name Kevin Stone. He'll be spending the night here. No, I don't know his plans for tomorrow."

Eric was shattered. He felt his bowels loosen, but he tightened his sphincter muscles, preventing such a reaction.

He staggered away from the door. He needed air. The apartment building was suffocating him. He hurried down the stairs and burst through the door and out into the night air.

He didn't hear Marsha say "Grandpa, I don't know why you're interested in him, but I like him very much." After a pause she said, "Yes, this soon. All I know is that he's special. So I won't be doing any spying for you anymore. I don't know what business you have with him. Maybe he's trying to get a big loan from you or something. I don't really care. But that's not my business so if you want to spy on him, you'll have to do it yourself."

Her grandfather assured her that he'd not be calling on her anymore for such assistance. At that moment he felt foolish over involving the girl in something like this. Maybe he was getting old and silly. Maybe even senile.

They told each other that they loved each other and wished

117

each other well before hanging up.

Eric's eyes were aflame with rage as he drove up Walnut Street. He turned on 52nd Street and approached a bar, Mr. Silk's Third Base Lounge. He rang the bell several times before a bulky black man came to the door.

"Whatchu want, man?"

"I want a bottle of champagne."

"Get the fuck away from here," the man said.

"Listen bitch, open this damn door and get me what I asked for before I fuck you up."

The man not only opened the door, he nearly ripped it off its hinges. Nobody talked to him like that.

"Bitch, huh?" He reached for Eric. "You called me a bitch?"

Eric's forward snap kick caught him in the groin. He bent over from the excruciating pain.

"Motha fuckah!"

The hulk stood up and swung a beefy black fist at Eric's face. Eric grabbed his wrist. His speed was greater by far than the sluggish moves of the larger man. Eric yanked the man's left arm toward himself with his right hand and, pulling the other man's arm, he swung with his hips, his back, his legs. He felt the impact of contact down to his toes. He heard something in the man's jaw crack. The huge bouncer fell softly to the pavement.

Eric walked in. The place was nearly empty. No after hours action tonight. Eric walked to the office in the back and saw that the proprietor was alone counting his night's receipts.

No wonder that monster was giving him a hard time. Well, fuck him. I got problems of my own, he thought.

Eric knew where the owner kept his private stash. He got a bottle, picked up some Virginia Slims cigarettes for his non-smoking girl friend, and left several bills on the counter.

118

Somebody would find the bouncer lying on the sidewalk and call an ambulance. Hopefully.

Schofield walked out and closed the door.

He drove off and headed back toward Marsha's apartment. He knocked softly on her door. She opened it.

Some girls looked better fully attired. Others were dazzling when scantily clad. A very few looked their best in the nude.

Marsha was nude. And she looked her best. At that moment Schofield knew that he'd never again see a creature more pleasing to the eye.

She looked glad to see him, as if he'd been gone for a long time. He gently closed the door. She stepped into his arms. He, still carrying the bottle and the cigarettes, wrapped his arms around her and kissed her passionately.

"I brought us a bottle," he said when their kiss finished. "I think we should celebrate."

"Champagne, no less!" said Marsha, smiling. "What are we celebrating?"

"Eternity," said Eric.

"Eternity? Wow! That's kind of heavy, isn't it? Eternity. I think I like the way that sounds."

Eric got two glasses and poured drinks for them both.

"You're still dressed!" Marsha exclaimed as though being clothed was, at best, ludicrous.

"Forgive me. I'm very sorry," said Eric with mock contrition.

"You take off your armor and I'll be back," Marsha said, walking into the bedroom.

Who are you, Eric thought. Who put you on me? I could have fallen in love with you. But you betrayed me and for that you'll die.

Marsha returned and Eric smiled sadly, detesting the task that lay ahead. She carried a small plastic jar filled with a scented oil. She switched off all the lights except a soft, red one that barely silhouetted their naked bodies. She turned on the stereo and Schofield sat down next to her.

Marsha sprinkled some of the oil onto her hands. The rose-like fragrance came into Eric's nostrils. Marsha rubbed Eric's back with it, applying gentle pressure to the long tight muscles. Eric stretched out on his stomach, enjoying the attention.

Major Harris' "Love Won't Let Me Wait" played on the stereo.

Now she was massaging his lower back in slow, almost painful strokes. Her hands slid over his buttocks and she allowed her fingernails to scratch lightly, producing a tingling sensation. She turned him over and blew softly on his nipples and, to his embarrassment, he felt arousal building and knew they were hardening. Now she licked them, first the right and then the left. She traced a trail down the center of his chest with her tongue. She slid to his belly and stuck her tongue inside his navel.

Eric usually tried to maintain his cool during sex. It was his intention to provide the pleasure and most of his came from giving it to his ladies. He made sure that he remained in complete control and had seldom even permitted himself the luxury of a sigh or a whispered endearment.

Growing up, all such displays were signs of weakness and although Eric knew that was silly, he had a hard time shaking the ancient taboos of his youth. But now his body writhed beneath the skilled manipulations of the strikingly beautiful girl above him. His abdominal muscles twitched involuntarily.

Now her lips were on his pubic hair. He reached down and grabbed her soft, dark hair and had to restrain himself from pulling it, yanking it clean out.

She ran her tongue around the head of his penis.

He gasped.

120

She opened her lips and enclosed him in her mouth.

"Lord have mercy!" The words were out before he could stop them.

Hours later she lay asleep atop him. He opened his eyes, fighting off the temptation to doze.

He touched her neck, felt the life flowing through her jugular vein. He reached for the back of her head. With his other hand he held her chin. One sudden snap and it would be over.

Schofield had experienced difficulty in killing before. Sometimes he'd had to get close to a person, be friendly with them for weeks before he could produce the right circumstance to facilitate their death.

This time it would be harder than it had ever been. Almost impossibly hard.

He felt like saying fuck it. Fuck the betrayal. In spite of it all he still wanted her. But he'd soon be a dead man if he did business like that.

Softly he kissed her forehead then braced his muscles for the snap.

"I have something to tell you." Her voice, tired and satisfied, shocked Schofield. He thought she was in deep sleep. He released his hands. Another second and she would've been dead.

Part of his mind told him to kill her, not give her a chance to fully awaken because he might not be able to do it if he had to look into her eyes, see the shock and pain.

His arms stiffened at his side.

"I deceived you. I'm so sorry," she said. "I tried to meet you on purpose. I knew you'd be at the library. My grandfather wanted me to get to know you. He said you might be moving away, but that he hoped you'd let me know where you were going. I was then supposed to tell him.

"I know Kevin Stone isn't your real name. Grandpa said

121

you had another name but he didn't tell me what it was. Wanted me to use 'Kevin' naturally, so you wouldn't suspect anything.

"Baby, I don't know what kind of business you have with my grandfather. Maybe he loaned you some money and you're trying to get out of paying it back. I don't care! I don't care what it is. All I know is that something has happened to me. I guess it may sound corny, but I knew when I first saw you that you were a man different from any I've ever met before in my life.

"I'm in love with you and I don't want to do anything that'll hurt you in the least."

She stopped, breathing hard. Eric said nothing.

"I called him," she said when she'd gotten her breath back. "I'm so ashamed. I feel so...so *dirty*.

"I told him that I'd never spy on you again. I don't want to lose you. But if you don't want me anymore, if you don't want to see me again..."

The relief hit Schofield like a flood, almost wiping him out. He looked into her dark eyes. Her tears were falling on his face. They formed rivers that rolled down his cheeks.

Chapter Ten

Isaac Payne had serious questions about the wisdom of his usage of Marsha to keep an eye on Schofield. Even if he couldn't use the vast resources of the Guardian Angels, he wondered if there wasn't some other way he could've kept tabs on Pisces.

He reflected on the conversation he'd had with Marsha the night before. She really sounded like she'd been touched deeply by the killer. She had no idea of the danger she'd be in if she divulged a word to Schofield. He'd think nothing of killing her.

Yes, he had been foolish. He was overstepping his range with this double-agent role. He had check writing power with the Guardian Angels, but that extra-cautious Jacob Robb would only track down the expenditure and possibly learn that he'd had Schofield followed. He was even afraid to utilize his own assets. Who could tell when Jacob Robb, already seemingly suspicious, would use his banking connections to find out how Payne had been spending his money?

Things were so touchy now. Any large cash withdrawals would surely raise questions. The other Guardian Angels knew he was for Farrakhan, not Wallace. So they were apt to be suspicious of whatever he did.

And of course he could not tail Schofield himself. Even if he was physically able, Schofield knew him and if he were spotted that could mean his life.

He hadn't had much time to arrange a plan for stopping Schofield. He didn't know when he'd pull out of Philadelphia for Chicago. So he had had to make an immediate connection. His reasoning was that if Marsha, his granddaughter, caused Schofield to become attached to her, he'd give her a periodic phone call even while stalking his quarry in Chicago. He would have Marsha's phone tapped and hopefully he would be able to trace Schofield's calls and learn of his whereabouts.

It was dangerous, but not a bad plan, he thought smugly, for a spur of the moment thing. Judging from Schofield's insatiable appetite for the softer gender and the psychological profile he'd had Joseph Malcolm prepare, Schofield was ripe for a meaningful relationship. Even in Schofield's many casual affairs there had been element of real emotional involvement. Sex, to Schofield, was never an end unto itself. Rather it was an effort to recapture some of the emotional warmth that death had snatched away from him.

Schofield, he knew, needed women. He needed to share conversation and feeling with them. Which was the real reason why he retained Tracey Bivens as his agent. He surrounded himself with women.

Unlike other G.I.'s, Schofield had had little opportunity to sample the Vietnamese women. His tour was almost celibate. Such a condition makes for reactions similar to those of a person who has undergone incarceration. The opposite sex takes on a greater than usual importance.

Schofield had found what his heart desired in Laura. But after Laura died, leaving him partially empty, he'd tried to fill the void with a series of affairs. His very decision to become an assassin was reaction to his guilt feelings regarding Laura's death.

At least, Yusuf Malik had indicated as much.

Yes, Schofield would stay in contact with Marsha. He would call from Chicago. Things would work out. Isaac Payne was certain of it.

Payne had called his granddaughter immediately following the predawn fajr prayer. Marsha had answered the phone sleepily. He hung up. She was alive. That was all he wanted to find out. Evidently, she hadn't said anything to Schofield. Therefore, everything could proceed as planned. A lonely Schofield would call his newly found girl friend and he, Ishaq Bayan, would have his number and location.

Ishaq Bayan knew how Abraham the prophet must have felt. Abraham had been directed by an angel to slay his own son. A student of scriptural symbolism, Ishaq knew Abraham's ''son'' represented his works. Abraham had to tear down what he had himself erected in order to progress further in God's cause.

Issac Payne was prepared, like Abraham, to destroy the work he'd helped the Guardian Angels to produce during four decades of meticulous labor. The most vital objective of the Guardian Angels was to one day be in a position to determine who would lead the Nation of Islam into the twenty-first century.

After so much work and so many years, they were finally able to insure their selection.

The laborers in the Nation referred to Elijah's office as ''Moses' seat.'' And these four men, virtually forgotten by

125

Elijah soon after Fard's departure, were capable of hand-picking the man who would next occupy that seat.

But what irony! They had chosen the wrong man.

In the mythological teachings of Master Fard Muhammad, the twenty-four scientists were the men who controlled the world. They had decided to destroy America for her sins. One of them opposed immediate destruction because black people were there. This dissident felt it was unjust for the poor ex-slaves to receive punishment for the crimes white people alone had committed.

The other scientists felt that blacks were "too far gone." They could not be reformed and "returned to their own kind." But the one man disagreed and set out to save Black America and to prove the others wrong.

That dissident was Master Fard Muhammad and, by his foresight and rebellion he proved himself superior to his colleagues and they would eventually have to recognize him as "the supreme ruler of the universe."

Isaac had to smile at his own egotistical thoughts. Unconsciously he had been equating himself with the Saviour, Master Fard Muhammad. And he knew he was not the equal of that man. Yet there were definite parallels between his dissent from the Guardian Angels and that of Fard from the twenty-four scientists of Mecca.

Tel Aviv, Israel

Martin Kahn spit an orange seed into the wastepaper basket. He was excited, "charged up" as his American friends would say.

When he was first approached, right out of college, to work for MOSSAD, he'd had visions of trotting around the globe using an assortment of exotic weapons to crush the hidden enemies of the State of Israel. He saw himself climbing into a variety of beds—in the line of duty of course—with myriad foreign beauties a la James Bond.

He was an acknowledged computer wizard at the age of nineteen. Even while in college, officers from the Army brought problems to him for solving. He found them simple and, in retrospect, he believed they were really only testing him to see if he'd be of any future use to the Israeli intelligence community.

He was twenty-one when he started working with MOSSAD. But, instead of making him a glamorous field agent, they'd stuck him inside a building with a million computers where he was one of numerous nameless nobodies who compiled ridiculous information like the projected weather forecast for Nairobi, Kenya, on a certain date way in the future.

They even had to record the expected level of skirt hemlines in the United States for a particular year! What had any of this to do with Israel's security? What good had the weeks of training been? He had top security clearance, was nominally a MOSSAD agent, and saw about as much action as a clerk typist who banged keys for a Hassidic rabbi.

Today they even had him filing folders! Miriam, a co-worker, had taken sick and he had to help out with her workload which consisted mainly of filing new material before it could be computerized.

Look at this shit. Eyes only! Eyes only! Top secret! This is a damn joke. Probably something discovered about zinc in New Hampshire or something very relevant to our security like that, he thought.

In mockery, Martin Kahn began opening folders and reading a passage before, with a sardonic chuckle, filing them in the huge metal cabinet.

"Cigarette prices to rise in Britain . . ." he read to himself. He placed a few folders into the cabinet then randomly selected another. He read: "Investigate Italian comedian who makes filthy jokes about Israeli officials." He seriously considered dumping the whole batch of worthless papers inside a trash can and quitting on the spot.

He, almost hysterical now, reached for another file.

"Ambassador Yacob's assassin believed to be code named Pisces," he read.

Derisively, Kahn filed the folder with the others.

Then it hit him. What was that he'd just read?

He dug back into the cabinet and yanked out the folder. He read again: "Ambassador Yacob's assassin believed to be code named Pisces. Information incomplete. Contractors: U.S.A. No specific department known. Retaliatory actions recommended: None. Related events: PLO guerrilla base struck. Conclusion: Some party in U.S.A. acted to prevent Yacob from obtaining financing for a possible new Mid-East conflict."

Martin Kahn was impervious to the sound of the folder striking the floor after his hand went limp and his mouth opened weakly.

This was incredible.

Eric Schofield had been to a lot of picnics in his life, but this one, right in Fairmount Park, would be indelibly ingrained in his memory.

He dug into the ripe watermelon with his fork.

"Oh, you're so prim and proper," laughed Marsha. "You don't eat watermelon with a fork. Where'd you grow up?"

"I don't like burying my face in it; reminds me of something else," he said.

"Oh really? That's a surprise to me. I didn't know you knew of such things, you prude."

"Is that supposed to make me feel guilty or what?" asked Schofield.

"Oh, I wouldn't think of implying. . . ." Marsha left the

sentence hanging.

Without any warning Eric's mood shifted and Marsha picked up on it immediately.

"Sometimes you have to save the best for last," he said somberly.

"Last? What last?" she asked.

"I have to leave town."

"Leave town? Why? Where? Where are you..."

She was stricken. He had become an important, very important, part of her life, of her plans.

"Kevin, this is terrible. Unless...you'll be right back, won't you?"

"I'm not sure, honey," said Eric, shattering her hopes. "It'll be at least a month. Probably more."

Schofield felt terrible. He should've just pulled out and split. He wasn't good with goodbyes. But he just couldn't leave without some sort of explanation.

"Let me see if I'm getting this right. What you're saying is that this is it. Finished. A few weeks and it's bye-bye. Have I got it right?"

"No, Marsha."

"Oh yes! I'm right and you know it! Here I was falling in love with you and, for you, it was nothing. Nothing! Wham, bam and thank you ma'am."

"Marsha! Marsha! Just wait a second, will you? I feel as much as you feel for me." He was holding her shoulders, talking directly into her face.

"I have something I have to take care of," he continued. "It may take a month, maybe more. It's not inconceivable for it to take half a year. But I won't forget you, ever. I'll be back. You gotta believe me baby. You gotta trust me."

"I'll come with you then," said Marsha.

"You can't. Really, you can't."

"Why? You have a wife waiting for you somewhere? Is

that it?''

''Boy! How I wish it was that simple! No, sweetheart. I have to take care of some business, business that was arranged before I even met you. I can't tell you any more about it. I have to ask you to trust me; beg you to trust me, because I don't want you to give up on me. I don't want to lose you.

''Besides,'' he added after several moments, ''you have to start the semester soon and you can't just stop like that.'' He mussed her hair and looked at her. She was painfully beautiful.

''Fuck the semester,'' she said.

''Little girl, you have the beauty of Cleopatra but the mouth of a sailor.''

''I'm serious, Kevin. I can enroll after the Christmas break.''

''Marsha, you're just gonna have to trust me. I'll be back. I *will* be back. I'd love to have you with me. I'm just that selfish. I'm glad you put being with me ahead of school. But what I have to do has to be done alone. You are just going to have to accept that.''

Still as a statue, she sat on the soft green earth, her eyes squeezed shut. She refused to open the passageway for the tears which pressed against her eyelids to roll out.

''You have something dangerous to do, don't you, Kevin?'' She didn't wait for his response. ''I don't have any idea what all you're into. I don't really care. I mean it doesn't affect...it can't stop my loving you, no matter what it is. But I know I'll be worried out of my mind for weeks, for months if you take that long. I won't even know if you're alive or...or...''

The tears sprang from her eyes. Her face was contorted in confusion and pain.

Eric Schofield loved this girl and he was tortured by her

130

pain and the very thought of her agonizing over him for all the weeks he'd be gone.

"I don't know what I can do, Marsha," he said weakly.

"Will you at least call me? At least let me know you're all right?

This wasn't going as he had planned. He had lost control of the situation.

"Yeah. I'll call. Not every day, but I'll call you now and then. I won't put you through that."

He spent that night with her.

Alone, in the privacy of her apartment, they danced together. They poured wine for each other. They listened to each other's childhood memories and adult fantasies. They tried to cram years of intimacy into a single night.

Somehow each of them felt the very real possibility that this might turn out to be their last night together.

Marsha confessed that she had been taking guitar lessons. She had always wanted to play an instrument, so for the past year she'd been taking lessons.

Eric wanted to hear her play.

"Oh no! I'm really terrible."

But he goaded her until she finally relented.

It turned out that she had been right. Her playing was horrible.

But it was the most melodic sound Eric's ears had ever heard.

Then she sang. A soulful version of the Beatles' "Long and Winding Road." Her singing was special, ten hundred times better than her guitar playing.

While singing she allowed herself to cry. And there, in plain view of the woman he had begun to love, Eric Schofield cried too.

When they went to bed that night, Eric ate watermelon for the second time. This time, however, he didn't use a fork.

131

Chapter Eleven

Most members of Chicago's Muhammad's Temple of Islam No. 2 faithfully did their banking at the Muslim's newly purchased Guaranty Bank and Trust.

The ownership of a bank had long been a goal of the Honorable Elijah Muhammad, so it would be an affront to him if his own followers didn't bank at the institution he'd labored so relentlessly to secure.

Gwendolyn Akbar did her banking there. She recalled the euphoric mood that swept the Messenger's home when the bank had finally been purchased. For the first time that she knew of, the usually stern Messenger had told the sisters to dance. Shocked at his deviation from protocol, they hesitated.

"Dance, sisters," he ordered. "This is a time for celebration. Allah has fulfilled His promise to His Messenger."

Now, though, there was no gaiety in Sister Gwendolyn's

mood. There wasn't any one thing that was bothering her. Rather, there was a host of nagging things that resulted in her melancholy mood.

She stood in line, waiting to cash her check.

"As-Salaam-Alaikum, Sister Gwendolyn," an elderly brother spoke.

"Wa-Alaikum Salaam, Brother Theodore. How are you?" She tried to present a sunny disposition.

"Oh fine, all praise is due to Allah and his Messenger." The old brother walked jauntily past her and out the door.

Gwendolyn Akbar was one of the secretaries of the Honorable Elijah Muhammad and, in the Nation of Islam, there was no more prestigious position that a woman could hold.

Along with several other of the Messenger's secretaries, Gwendolyn lived at the leader's mansion at 4855 South Woodlawn Avenue. She was treated with a reverence by fellow Muslims that puzzled her. It was as though the minute she'd gotten the job she became holy or something to them. But whenever she checked the mirror, she was unable to find any halos hovering over her head. She was the same Gwendolyn she'd always been, as far as she could see.

It was her turn to cash her check.

"As-Salaam-Alaikum, Sister Akbar."

"Wa-Alaikum Salaam, Sister Dorine. I'd like to deposit $50.00 in my savings account and have the rest in cash, please." She handed her the check and the deposit slip.

"How's Dear Apostle?" the teller asked.

"He's doing fine. His health has never been better. All praise is due to Allah. How're your children?" Gwen inquired.

"Fine. Fine. Bad as can be, though. I just worry about the school." She leaned forward and whispered, "I've been thinking about putting them in the public school. It's hard

133

to afford the University of Islam, and there are some basic skills they seem to be missing.''

"Now Sister Dorine," said Gwen, "that would break Dear Apostle's heart. You know that. Sometimes we have to make sacrifices. We're trying to build a nation, sister.''

Gwendolyn felt her stomach tighten. Dorine was right. She did have nerve telling her to make sacrifices. She had probably made ten times the sacrifices that she, Gwendolyn, had made. She was raising two children alone on a bank teller's salary, plus paying that sky high tuition for the children at the school. She felt ashamed.

"You're probably right. It is easier for me to talk. Maybe you should talk to Minister Shah. Perhaps they can arrange something for you on the tuition. If that doesn't work, give me a call at The House. I'll try to get you in to see the Messenger. I know he can help you.''

Dorine's face beamed. "Sister Gwendolyn, I would really appreciate that! I'll take your advice. Do you really think I might be able to see the Messenger?''

"The Messenger is here to help us. If he can get the time in his schedule, I'm sure he'll want to see you. That's how he is. But first see Minister Shah. Then, if necessary, we'll try to get you in to see the Messenger.''

After exchanging greetings again, Sister Gwendolyn walked out of the bank onto Stoney Island Avenue. Dorine 23X looked after her for a moment. Gwen was so much different from those other secretaries who worked at The House. Most of them were so haughty and proud and they spoke in a sneering manner to the other sisters. Gwen wasn't like that. She was everyday people.

Sister Gwendolyn started her red Audi Fox and merged into the traffic on Stoney Island. She thought about her conversation with Sister Dorine. She was displeased with herself for handing Dorine the standard line of baloney that they fed all the poor believers when things got rough. Goodness! She hoped she wasn't becoming like the rest of them. Sometimes the people in authority acted like they didn't give a damn about the common believers.

Her Audi took a sharp turn and she headed toward Your Supermarket on Cottage Grove. She loved her little Fox and she remembered the flack some sisters had given her when she'd purchased it. Red, they said, was too loud a color and attracted too much attention. One sister remarked that the Messenger had refused to walk on a red carpet once, preferring a white one. "I don't walk on blood, I walk on righteousness," the Messenger had reportedly said. But the Fox was the first brand new car that she had ever owned and she wasn't about to part with it or like it any less regardless of how much those nasty old hens cackled.

She didn't really fit in, she knew. For some reason she never had. She loved the Messenger tremendously. He was everything to her. But the atmosphere around him didn't agree with her nature.

The excitement of being one of his secretaries had worn off. It was a job now, and one that failed to inspire her. She was sick of the hypocrisy she'd witnessed among some of the secretaries. When the Messenger was not around they quarreled and bickered like a bunch of angry cats. They gossiped about one another, about the wives of Elijah's ministers, about the ministers themselves, and they viewed new sisters converted to the faith as threats to their high and mighty positions.

But whenever the Messenger entered the room, they suddenly became sugary sweet and rosy. They spoke no ill of anyone. Everything was simply beautiful.

Gwendolyn hated their hypocrisy. She'd been a full-time secretary for more than a year now, but before that she'd often filled in temporarily during periods, like Saviour's Day, when voluminous amounts of work had to be done.

But other things troubled Gwendolyn. She was twenty-six years old and still unmarried. She felt that being one of the Messenger's secretaries scared a lot of brothers away from her. And the few brothers who were caring enough to venture past that holy aura that surrounded the secretaries were not at all the kind of men who appealed to her.

Living at The House, she was not in a position to meet many single brothers. Most of the people who came to the home of the Apostle were ministers, captains, and Temple secretaries from around the country. Ninety percent of these were married. Yet she had noticed, on several occasions, esteemed ministers leering at her lecherously.

She was tired of being cooped up in that house twenty-four hours a day. She felt life was leaving her in the lurch. She hardly even attended Temple meetings anymore. Increasingly, the duties of other sisters were being hoisted upon her shoulders. She found herself carrying more than her own workload. Often she plugged on into the late evening with office work that should've already been done.

What am I, some sort of Rapunzel or Cinderella or somebody? I should just quit. Probably won't anyone notice, not even the Messenger, she thought.

Well, somebody had to look after the Messenger. Somebody who really cared. Ever since Sister Clara's death, the Apostle had been increasingly less in charge of things, delegating more and more authority to others. Much of his vigor seemed to have disappeared. He seemed more frequently hobbled with ailments, more than ever like a tired old man.

Well, at least I can get my own apartment. I need some privacy. This place is smothering me. I can get my own place.

Brother Phillip 17X worked part time at the Muslim-owned

136

Your Supermarket. He was dumping out trash when he saw Gwen's red Audi Fox pull into the parking lot. Phillip was eighteen years old and would be leaving for college in a matter of weeks.

The driver of that Audi would be one of the many things about Chicago that Phillip would miss. For years Phillip had had a crush on Gwendolyn Akbar, as did many young members of the FOI. He watched Gwendolyn Akbar step out of the car. He observed her striding gracefully, and he felt his heart flutter. He marvelled at her beauty.

It was against the Messenger's teachings to look lustfully at the sisters, but of late Phillip had been having an extremely difficult time keeping lustful thoughts from his mind when he saw Sister Gwendolyn.

Gwendolyn Akbar was nearly six feet tall. But despite being statuesque she had a soft, vulnerable manner about herself. Her face was more rounded than angular, giving her a kind appearance. Her huge brown eyes told how she really felt no matter how she tried to keep her feelings from showing. Phillip could always tell when she was really feeling fine or when her words—"Fine, praise be to Allah"—simply masked her true emotional state.

Often Phillip had tried to build up the courage to speak to her about his feelings, but he was afraid she'd either laugh or dismiss him kindly as a boy struck with a bad case of puppy love.

He finished dumping the huge barrels of trash and rushed in so that he could take his usual position as a cashier. Maybe Gwendolyn would check out at his counter.

As Gwendolyn shopped she reflected upon her work as Messenger Muhammad's secretary. One of the major reasons Gwendolyn had taken the position was to be privy to his nightly "table talks," the wisdom he shared with his followers around the dinner table. But of late the Apostle

137

seemed too tired to do much talking, and when he did feel up to entertaining, the more powerful secretaries seemed to always succeed in getting table seats while Gwen was relegated to kitchen chores.

If she got her own apartment, the Messenger, in all likelihood, wouldn't even know she'd left.

In this mood, Gwendolyn shopped for the Messenger of Allah's home. She was so wrapped in her own thoughts that she forgot to even speak to the nice young brother, Phillip, who waited on her at the counter.

She remembered after she'd started up her car and recalling now the disappointed look on the brother's face, she got out and dashed back into the supermarket.

"Brother Phillip," she called, "I hear you're going away to school. I just want to wish you all the success in the world. The Messenger needs talented brothers like you."

If Brother Phillip's grin was any wider, she thought, the whole top of his head might fall off.

"Y-yes, ma'am. Yes ma'am," was all Phillip could manage.

Gwendolyn smiled to herself when she was back in her car. She remembered her own first crush when she was a teenager. When Phillip got settled at school he'd meet girls his own age and forget his little crush. She was pleased with the thought.

Ya'qub Rabb, known as Jacob Robb in the financial world, left the Bankers Trust branch in Times Square. He still had plenty of time before his appointment with the mayor. He would recommend measures to divert the city from its present course of financial suicide.

Robb was accustomed to politicians seeking his advice. He was equally accustomed to them ignoring every bit of advice he offered. He could tell that a mental block arose

138

in their minds whenever he spoke to them. They were incapable of really taking his counsel. They were too preoccupied with the hue of his skin. Yet they inevitably sought him. He knew that the real motive was to demonstrate to their black constituents that minority financial concerns were of great importance to them. After all, hadn't the advice of a ranking black economist been sought?

But none of this ritualistic political dancing bothered Ya'qub much. After so many years of it he was used to the reactions he caused in white politicians. These days he found it all mildly amusing.

He was glad they only took him half seriously. That made it easier for him to continue his divine work, the work of removing the white man, ultimately, from every position of power on the earth.

It was long, tedious and complicated work. Ya'qub didn't delude himself into thinking he'd see the fruition of his work in his lifetime. But over the decades white world power would be gradually replaced by that of black people. First, though, the myth of white spiritual superiority—that psychological advantage that has spurred a pathetic minority on to world domination over the vast majority—had to be destroyed.

He pondered over the words of Paul: "We battle not against flesh but against principles, and spiritual wickedness..."

The real power of the white man was not his gun, but his principle, the hidden message in the Trinitarian doctrine: *The White Man is God.*

Master Fard Muhammad understood. He met the problem head on: *The White Man is the Devil and the Black Man is God.*

Reverse psychology. And it was gradually working. Black people now viewed white people's deeds through that axiom.

Some whites were even interpreting themselves through that filter!

Elijah also understood. Now, at least, he did. Not before, but it was clear that he understood now. He spoke of "the battle in the sky," meaning the war to establish principles in the mind. In his book *The Fall of America,* he'd written that the Mothership—the flying saucer designed to destroy white America—really represented the Last Messenger. So he'd finally learned that there is no huge saucer hovering about in outer space waiting to bomb white America and to redeem the black man. The message will accomplish that. The truth will set you free.

Still, Ya'qub Rabb was troubled. He was nagged by a dull ache that refused to go very far away.

He was disturbed that the very man who did not support the choice the Guardian Angels had made was the man they'd selected to see that their man was brought to the throne.

Rabb didn't trust Ishaq's abilities. Over forty years he'd proved himself, time and again, to be a man of remarkable capabilities. Rabb wondered if a man so convinced that the choice of Wallace was wrong would, or even could, act to assure that the very person he felt was unqualified would be placed on the throne.

Ironically, none of the Guardian Angels were very close on a personal level. They were drawn together over a common commitment, an agreement on how the design of the Saviour had to be implemented. The very fact that they were *not* close perhaps had accounted for their staying united in the work for forty years.

Personal attachments led to disputes based more upon emotions than logic.

Ishaq Bayan, Jacob thought, was convinced that Farrakhan was the best man for the post. He didn't just feel that way, he was certain of it.

140

How could a man see the work of a lifetime culminate in the wrong selection? Indeed, how could he?

Elijah Muhammad had designed a system that his secretaries were to use in responding to letters from his followers. As most of their questions had been asked many times previously, the Messenger had the replies filed according to subject matter. In this way, most questions could be answered by reproducing the Messenger's previous response.

Most letters to Mr. Muhammad could be answered in that manner. There were files for answering questions on poetry, Arabic names, entertainment, sports, polygamy, cigarette smoking, non-Muslim spouses, and every area his many followers were concerned with during Elijah's mission.

However, most of the secretaries had grown too indolent over the years to research the answers in order to prepare a response from the Messenger's own words. They usually elected to answer off the cuff, attempting to imitate the Messenger's terse letter writing style.

The secretaries in the letter writing department had a quota of twenty-five letters per day to answer. Gwendolyn Akbar was one of the few who religiously researched all the questions to give each writer an answer from the Apostle's own words. As a result, she sometimes fell short of the quota of twenty-five letters.

Rosalyn Bey walked to Gwendolyn's desk.

"How many letters have you gotten out, Sister?" asked the senior secretary of the staff.

"Thirteen, Sister Rosalyn," replied Gwen.

"It's nearly four o'clock. The Messenger's dinner is to be ready by six. How are you going to prepare the meal when you haven't even completed your quota?"

"Sister, it takes time finding the right answers. Besides,

141

I had to go shopping." When Rosalyn didn't speak, Gwen said, "I've been having trouble with this letter." She pointed to a handwritten letter on her desk. "It's on a very sensitive subject and I haven't been able to find a proper answer. Maybe we should show it to Dear Apostle."

"Let me look at it," Rosalyn said.

Rosalyn was in her late forties, but she was energetic and strongly built. She reminded Gwendolyn of a female drill sergeant. She succeeded wonderfully at intimidating the newer secretaries. Rosalyn had been with the Messenger for twenty years.

"Nancy," she called, "come over here. You gotta hear this."

Nancy Salaam was her lieutenant and alter ego. She'd worked for the Messenger for ten years herself. They served as each other's only friends on the secretarial staff.

Nancy came eagerly over to Gwen's desk. She knew that Rosalyn didn't have kind feelings for Gwen. Rosalyn didn't care for any of the new breed of slick college girls who were flocking to the Nation. They came to get men, not for righteousness or even out of strong faith. They came for the brothers.

Nancy and Rosalyn had been Muslims during the harsh, lonely years when it took courage to proclaim Islam as your faith. Yet, despite their record of dedication, neither of them had ever married.

But these new girls were prancing the Temples and snaring husbands within weeks.

"Listen to this," said Rosalyn to Nancy: "'Dear Holy Apostle, my wife is giving me much trouble. She keeps staying out late at night and I know good Muslim sisters are not supposed to act like that. I don't know what to do. I love her and I don't want a divorce. But I feel like I'm getting disrespected around the house. Please help me, Dear Holy

Apostle. We have three children. Well, they were hers, but now that we're married I feel like they are mine too. As-Salaam-Alaikum, Brother Alonzo 21X.'''

Nancy and Rosalyn laughed violently. Gwendolyn just stared at them, confused and hurt. She saw nothing comical about the letter. Obviously, the man who wrote it was distressed by what was happening. How could these sisters be so heartless? Where was the compassion for a fellow Muslim follower of the Honorable Elijah Muhammad?

"Honey," said Rosalyn to Gwen, "here's how you answer this."

She spread her massive buttocks over Gwen's chair and began typing on her typewriter.

"Dear Brother," she wrote, "Obviously you have the disease of hypocrisy in your heart. Your hypocrisy has blinded you to the fact that your wife has suffered many hardships and should not be treated like a prisoner by you. Allah has blessed you with a good wife and you should show your appreciation by trusting her. Pray, brother, that Allah saves you from being fuel for the fire. As-Salaam-Alaikum, Elijah Muhammad, Messenger of Allah."

She signed the Messenger's name. Then she and Nancy convulsed with laughter.

Nancy said, "Wait'll that fool gets *this!* He'll probably cut his wrists. Damn fool."

Gwendolyn just stood there, dumbfounded. Rosalyn said to her, "Go on and prepare Dear Apostle's dinner. I'll answer the rest of your letters. I feel sharp today."

Gwendolyn struggled to keep a rein on her emotions. But when she was alone in the kitchen she lost control. Her tears fell into the Messenger's bean soup.

Colonel Abraham Micah eyed the young man suspiciously. Micah had been retired from MOSSAD for more than a year

143

and he wasn't anxious to get involved again in its activities.

"What you have told me is quite extraordinary," he said.

"But it's true, sir. Every word of it," Martin Kahn said.

Micah had been in espionage long enough to know that the recruiting officer took on a father-figure image to the person recruited. In fact, Israeli intelligence encouraged them to maintain that image. Therefore, he wasn't surprised when an excited, frightened and angered Martin Kahn came calling on him at his home.

The first thing he did was make the young man calm down. He fixed a cup of coffee for him. Then he told the computer expert to slowly explain everything that was troubling him. He was not to exclude a single detail.

After Kahn had finished, the Colonel said, "I shall check into this in the most minute detail." There was an unspoken threat in his words.

"All of it's true," repeated Kahn. "What are you going to do, sir? And will I be able to help you?"

"First things first, young man. No need to be hasty. But if there is any truth to what you say, *we* won't be the ones to relax our commitment to Israeli security. Of that you can be sure. The Law of Moses prevails."

The young man was a bit frightened by the tone of the Colonel's voice.

"What do you mean, sir? What Law of Moses?"

"A life for a life. Yesterday. Today. Always."

Chapter Twelve

Paris, France
September, 1974

Guillaume never pretended to understand why particular night spots became the "in" places among the international jet set. Nor did he pretend to understand why joints that were "what's happening" today became a total drag the next day.

He was just happy and felt lucky that his place, *Sputnik*, was presently the discotheque that attracted the big spenders throughout Europe, America, Africa and, more recently, the Arab world.

Black lights flashed, bodies gyrated, and the walls—responding to the thumping beat—pulsated. They were adorned with huge blown-up photographs of the first earth vehicle to enter outer space, the Russian *Sputnik*.

Guillaume wasn't a space buff. He just thought he needed a naughty title for the disco he intended to open. He wanted something anti-establishment, but hip. He considered dancing a form a rebellion, whether against husband, wife, society or acne pimples. You shook your rump in spite of it all and against your personal Pharaoh, even if Pharaoh was your own inhibitions.

A record by the American funk group Parliament-Funkadelic provided the devastating beat. A shrill female voice screamed over the record: "Get up for the downstroke! Everybody get up!"

Guillaume was making his regular tour of his disco, casually making certain that everything was in order. He wanted his guests to be free to have fun, but he knew that even great fun had to be limited or it would give way to chaos. And that was a downer and therefore bad for business.

A little discreet coke snorting here and there didn't phase him. Nor did the overflowing scent of marijuana. He just wanted to be sure nothing transgressed the bounds of "good, clean and unclean fun."

Sputnik had been chosen as a name because of the subtle tones of rebellion the name implied. It was Russian, whereas the dancers were either Westerners or citizens of countries whose governments had close ties with the West. Even the name's connection with outer space helped the dancer say, "Fuck it all. Fuck the whole planet earth."

This year, *Sputnik* was not only The Place, it was The Only Place, and Guillaume—tall, sharp featured, dark haired with a hint of subdued treachery—was becoming quite rich. He was the quintessential disco owner.

Musa Mahmoud was forty-five if he was a day. And watching him spinning through the crowd, dancing uncoordinatedly, was hilarious to behold. His wine glass was held high and it generously showered bystanders with its contents. The lights bounced off his balding pate as he bumped to the beat with reckless abandon.

To Musa Mahmoud, coming to Paris was like escaping from prison. Sure, Egypt wasn't as religiously strict as Saudi Arabia or Libya, but it was still a country that took Islam seriously.

A man was expected to make his five daily prayers. He was expected to attend the Friday *Juma'a* prayer service.

Musa had a wife and three children. He had an image to maintain. Beyond a doubt he loved his native Egypt (which he and his countrymen called *Misr*). But after spending several months at home, his native culture fitted him like a straitjacket. Therefore, he occasionally needed to place some distance between himself and his moralistic nation.

Paris was freedom. Here people lived and forgot tradition, image and moral standards. They were not angels, but human beings. Women were in abundance. All kinds. All nationalities. The world's finest beverages. A mind-blowing nightlife.

Musa worked hard at everything he did. Presently he was hard at work enjoying himself. And he recognized that he was being highly successful. He was having a ball.

Stevie Wonder's "Boogie On Reggae Woman" jumped out at Musa and he wriggled his plump ass to the thumping synthesizer. A large red wine stain colored his shirt over his rounded, bouncing belly.

Gay Paris! And Musa had almost forgotten the peculiar murders that had occurred this month. Two men who lived very far from him, but who were professionally very much like him, had been executed.

In Zurich a man had been murdered. An ice pick had been thrust savagely past his eyeball and into his brain. The partial remains of another man, whose home was Lisbon, were located by a dog who, while searching for food, had knocked over a trash can. Pedestrians were startled and sickened when a well-known head rolled from the can and down the street, the eyes open wide and staring.

These men were big fish in the business euphemistically called the referral service. They were middlemen who contracted the international hit men and well-trained mercenaries for prospective, very rich clients.

The major procurers were not unknown in the shadowy world of international intrigue. But the unwritten rule was that one didn't muscle the procurers around, even after a significant hit. One might have some future need of their services oneself. Yet someone had seen fit to murder two of these valuable sacred cows.

Musa was worried. Scared shitless, to be quite candid. Somebody didn't give a fuck about the rules. Well, to hell with it. He was on vacation and in Paris, his favorite city. Whatever happened in Switzerland and Portugal was far removed from him.

Musa cut in to dance with a large-legged German girl whose halter top kept falling to reveal one massive white tit. Musa bumped and managed to get bumped by one of the globes. Coming up from a dip, he felt his knees weaken. His head was spinning and he had to stagger backwards to regain his balance.

Guillaume saw all this and was stepping in to suggest that Musa call it a night. The man was quite obviously drunk.

Before he could move, an elderly man with sharp Semitic features tapped him on the shoulder. "He's had far too much to drink," the slender man said to Guillaume avuncularly. "He always does this in Europe. Really, he's not much of a drinker."

"Do you know Musa?" Guillaume asked.

"Unfortunately, I do," smiled the man. "He's my son-in-law. I allowed him to drag me here to your country. Then he leaves me to twiddle my thumbs in the hotel."

"Oh," was all Guillaume said. Already his eyes were

checking other regions of the disco.

"I had hoped to sample your renowned hospitality," the older man was saying, "but it seems Musa has transgressed the limits of his body's capacity to consume. I'd better collect him and take him back to the hotel."

"Yes, I think you're right," Guillaume said. He was happy to have a potentially embarrassing situation removed from his hands. "Do you need me to secure a car?"

"No need, thank you. I am driving."

A red-headed American girl caught Guillaume's attention and he was off to see to her needs.

The elderly, but apparently well-conditioned, man had little trouble getting the drunk, staggering Musa out of the discotheque and into a waiting automobile.

They'd driven for several miles when the Mercedes 600 hit a large pothole jarring the passengers.

Musa woke up drowsily from his drunken stupor. "What? Where am I?" he asked.

"Go back to sleep," said Colonel Abraham Micah gently. "I'm taking you home."

"Home," murmured Musa pleasantly and fell back into his inebriated slumber.

Within minutes they arrived at a house one of Colonel Micah's friends had secured for his use.

Quarts of black coffee were shovelled down Musa's gagging throat. After several cups and multiple trips to the latrine, Musa regained sobriety.

Spitting on the thick carpet and blowing his nose, Musa demanded, "Who are you? Where am I? What do you want?"

"Good evening, Shaykh Mahmoud. Or should I say good morning? It is quite late."

"Who are you? What am I doing here?" His head throbbed. His brain pounded relentlessly against the walls of his skull.

"I have spent several days trying to locate you, Musa," said the Colonel, ignoring Musa's questions. "You are certainly an elusive one."

The Israeli attempted many times to light his pipe. When he finally succeeded, the rich aroma flooded the room.

"There are certain questions I'd like to ask you, Musa. I do hope you will oblige an old man and answer them. I know you are quite fluent in English, so I need not speak your language, need I?"

Musa shook his head slowly.

"Very well. I do not intend to spend more time than is necessary. Please answer me directly. Who is the man you hired to kill Ambassador Yacob?"

"Who are you?" Musa jumped from his chair. His head cleared rapidly of all remaining fog. The murdered arrangers in Zurich and Lisbon came instantly to mind.

"I am from MOSSAD," said Colonel Micah. "That is all you need to know."

Musa pissed in his pants.

"Answer my questions honestly, Musa, and you will live. One lie, and you will die. It is as simple as that."

Musa nodded his head furiously. He was ready to talk, to tell everything he knew. You just didn't play games with MOSSAD.

"I will ask you once more. Who is the man who killed Yacob?"

"An American. I don't know his name. He's black," said Musa.

"You hired a man whose name you do not know? Come now, Musa."

"No! Honestly! He came to me. Years ago. I met him years ago. I just know his code name. Pisces."

"And how do you reach him? Since you don't have his

name, what do you do, place an ad in the *New York Times?*"
Micah's voice reeked of sarcasm.

"No! No, nothing like that. He contacts me. Only when he wants to work does he contact me. I am not able to contact him."

"And what does this Negro look like?" asked Micah.

"I don't know," Musa replied.

"Musa Ibn Mahmoud, I shall surely kill you."

"I am not lying. Oh Allah, make him believe me! He comes to me in disguises. Sometimes an old man. Sometimes as a woman. Often as an Arab. Once as a blind man. I never know how he'll appear."

Colonel Micah said, "Tell me everything you do know about him. Every contract, every person who purchased a contract. Every penny paid to Pisces."

Two hours later Musa had finished. The young man who had accompanied Micah, Martin Kahn, was prepared to take Musa back to his hotel.

"You have been a big help to us, Shaykh Mahmoud," said the Colonel smiling stiffly.

"I have told you everything I know. Everything," said Musa. His head was hung low.

"Then you may leave," Micah said.

"Just like that?"

"Sure. Martin here will drive you back to the city."

They drove in silence. The small country roads were dark and threatening. Musa hadn't been awake for the ride in but he felt strongly that they were driving, not toward Paris, but deeper into the country.

"Are we lost?" Musa asked the driver in a weak and coarse voice.

The driver didn't reply and that only made Musa's worry increase.

Finally, they pulled off the road. The car stopped.

151

"Get out," ordered Martin Kahn.

"Whaa...where...what are you doing?"

"Get out!" Kahn repeated.

Then Musa saw the long Israeli-made gun with the ugly silencer attached.

Musa obeyed. The man pulled a whiskey bottle from beneath the seat of the car. He walked Musa into a wooded area off to the side of the road.

"Pour this onto yourself," he ordered Musa. The Arab was prepared to obey, thinking the young man intended to make him seem drunk. But why? Probably to leave him on a side street like a drunk. That way police would pay him no attention if he blabbed a story of abduction.

Thorough, very thorough these Israeli dogs, thought Musa.

Only when the contents struck his head, face and body did Musa recognize the scent of gasoline. Musa tried vainly to stop more of the deadly liquid from dousing his body.

"Barakallah," said the Israeli. Then he tossed a burning match in Musa's direction.

The spine-chilling scream that emanated from Musa's burning lips was unheard in the deep country by any sympathetic human ears.

Chapter Thirteen

The phrase "money talks and bullshit walks" came to Eric Schofield's mind as he walked out of the main Bell Telephone office in Philadelphia.

Obtaining the number which Marsha had called long distance had been surprisingly easy. The call had been placed to an Isaac Payne of 3 Howland Drive in Roxbury, Massachusetts.

Abraham Micah landed at Kennedy Airport in New York. He knew now that Pisces was an American black.

Pisces was obviously expertly trained, highly disciplined and incredibly intelligent. The intelligence was innate. The discipline could be self-developed. But there was but one place where the expert training was given—the military. And how many blacks were trained in espionage, demolition, assassination and all of the far-reaching, mind-boggling feats

Pisces was rumored to have performed? Not very many.

The man he sought was a military trained man. For most people it'd be nearly impossible to obtain a list of possible candidates. But when you were a close friend of the Secretary of Defense, you could get certain things done.

Gwendolyn Akbar looked critically at her new apartment and pronounced herself satisfied. She felt like she'd been given a new lease on life. She had never before realized just how suffocating the atmosphere had been at the home of the Honorable Elijah Muhammad.

She was ecstatic. And she didn't care if those hens at The House cackled until their throats got sore. She never knew how much she missed doing the simple things that an adult woman should be free to do.

Now she could listen to the music she wanted to hear; read the books she wanted to read without worrying over those hens' gossip. She could dress comfortably in her nightclothes if she desired instead of having to remain fully attired in long dresses at all hours of the day and night that she was awake. Because The House was almost constantly filled with visitors, the sisters could never really relax the strict M.G.T. dress code, not even at home.

Now, if she ever got truly interested in a brother, she had a place that she could talk in, one that provided more privacy than she could ever have at The House.

Of course the law governing the conduct of M.G.T. members dictated that a chaperon would have to be present if ever she did entertain a brother. She recognized the importance of such a law and she had no intentions of breaking it. You never knew what might happen alone with a brother. She wasn't ready to take any chances. She was, after all, only human. And it had been years since she'd been intimate with a man.

Chapter Fourteen

Pete Fisher's office was located on the second floor, directly above the Sunshine Dry Cleaners on the Grand Concourse in the Bronx. The hand-scrawled sign in the window read, "Peter Fisher, Private Investigator."

Inside the office, Fisher sat on a small secretary's chair behind a green metal desk. The desk was a General Services Administration castaway that Fisher had found. Fisher's three hundred pounds of flesh poured over the edges of the chair and the chair screeched in protest at Fisher's every movement.

Before him on the desk was a box of one dozen glazed doughnuts. A single pastry sat lonely in the box, a testimony to Fisher's remarkable powers of consumption.

"Damn broad," Fisher mumbled aloud between chews. He reached absently for a quart of milk to help wash down the doughnuts. "Always calling in fucking sick whenever

I fucking need her. Bet she's sick alright. Sick from over-consumption of protein.''

He was referring to his secretary, Maria Perez, a young Puerto Rican who'd been employed by Fisher for six months. She'd called in sick and left Fisher with office chores, a thing he detested.

Fisher had been in the investigation business for a year and he was just beginning to make ends meet. His name was starting to get around and, hopefully, he'd be able to leave the Bronx and move to Manhattan in another year.

He dialed the number to his twenty-four-hour answering service while he annihilated the remaining doughnut.

"Hey, honey. Me. Pete. Any calls during the night?"

The woman at the answering service read him his messages while Fisher jotted down the information she was giving him.

"Uh huh, uh huh. . .yeah. Yeah. This guy, Bob Morgan, he leave a number I can call him back at? Yeah. No number. Just said he'd be in at 9:30 sharp. Alright. Thank ya, honeybunch. Hey, you ever get tired of answering phones for peanuts and wanna job with adventure,''—he said "adventure" in a tone he thought was seductive—"then you just come and see old Petey, you here?"

She heard. She had heard it many times before. And she knew Pete couldn't afford to hire a cockroach at under minimum wage.

"Sure, Pete. If I ever want a change, I'll give you a ring."

Eric Schofield, his hair sprinkled with gray and his face doctored to add twenty years to his age, walked up the stairs beside the Sunshine Dry Cleaners.

He didn't bother to knock on the door of Fisher's office. He merely opened it and walked in. It was 9:30 A.M.

"Mr. Fisher? I'm Bob Morgan," he said, extending his hand. Pete Fisher stuck out his own pink, meaty paw.

156

"I trust you received my message," said Eric Schofield.

"Yeah. Pleased to meetcha, Mr. Morgan. Have a sit down."

Schofield looked apprehensively at the dirty brown sofa to which Fisher pointed. The sofa had seen better days, about ten years previously, and was correspondingly stained with an assortment of food particles. It smelled as though too many neglected babies had slept there, angry, wet and stinking.

"No thank you," Schofield said. I prefer to stand."

"Suit yourself," Fisher said, oblivious of his furniture's effect upon his guest. "What can I do you for?" Fisher laughed heartily at his selection of words, his massive belly shaking.

When Schofield failed to return his mirth, he stopped abruptly.

Schofield had chosen Peter Fisher for the sole fact that he was new in the business and because Eric was sure that he had not yet established ties with the local police. And certainly not with the FBI or the CIA.

While working for Army Intelligence Schofield had compiled a list of private detectives who supplemented their income by providing tidbits of information to various law enforcement agencies. His list had grown large enough to frighten him away from any private detective who had a big name in the business.

He had selected the fat slob he saw before him. Despite his despicable personal habits, Schofield had learned that Fisher was a good detective who conducted his work intelligently and conscientiously.

"I would like to employ your services. There is a man in Boston about whom I'd like to learn everything I can. I have his name, address and telephone number. I want you to discover what he's worth, who his friends and business associates are, what he does for kicks—everything about him.

157

Can you handle that?''

"Boston? Hey, what you're talking about takes bread, Mac. I don't work for gratis. Two bills a day plus expenses. And by expenses I mean airplane to and from Boston, no trains. Hotel expenses and car rental. And for what you want it'll take at least two weeks, maybe more. No offense, but not too many, uh, black guys can spend that kinda dough.''

"Allow me to worry about the 'dough,'" said Schofield. He clearly disliked the private detective.

"Well, you know that they say. Money talks. Bullshit walks." Fisher leaned back, belched and lit a cigar.

Schofield handed the man an envelope.

"There's five thousand dollars here. That should be sufficient to get you started.''

Sister Gwendolyn Akbar's situation at 4855 South Woodlawn Avenue had taken a turn for the better. Her recent independence, a rarity among Elijah Muhammad's secretaries, had made her a conversation piece among the other inhabitants of The House.

Even the Messenger himself seemed to be paying more attention to her. He'd personally instructed her to be present during a dinner in honor of a delegation from Peru. The Nation of Islam purchased hundreds of thousands of pounds of Whiting fish from the Peruvian government.

Rosalyn Bey and Nancy Salaam were not overjoyed with Gwen's ascending status. But they were cautious enough to refrain from their usual verbal abuse. They were careful not to arouse the displeasure of the Apostle.

When Messenger Muhammad announced that he was placing Sister Gwendolyn in charge of the letter answering department, her rapid ascension was officially stamped.

Eric Schofield landed in Chicago's O'Hare Airport and

took a cab into the city. He was using the name of Arthur Keefe and had obtained identification papers in that name.

There were several ways of obtaining false identification. One way was to pick a tourist's or a traveler's pocket at an airport. Often passports as well as driver's licenses and other I.D. were obtained by bumping a pedestrian and lifting his wallet which usually rode in the person's back pocket, the easiest place from which to remove it.

This time, however, Eric wasn't taking any chances. Arthur Keefe had been the name of a dead man. So, there was no way for the real Mr. Keefe to be billed by a car rental agency or a hotel for additional charges or sent sweepstakes tickets by a restaurant for being their one millionth customer or something like that.

Eric Schofield planned meticulously and he therefore seldom worried about failure. He did worry about freak accidents. Accidents like running into a man who knew the man whose I.D. was being utilized. "Morton Ferguson? Wow! My uncle's name is..."

He could not afford, at such a late stage, an event like that. So, Schofield had located the name of a person who had died many years ago but who, had he lived, would have been approximately his own age. He had obtained his birth certificate months ago by merely writing for it. He then obtained a driver's license and a passport. Officially, he *was* Arthur Keefe.

As the taxi pushed on toward the city Schofield mentally outlined his plans for the next few days.

His first order of business was to secure an apartment several miles away from Elijah Muhammad's home.

Schofield knew that as soon as the bullet struck Elijah's skull both the police and the FOI would investigate every place in the vicinity of Elijah's mansion. Of course, neither of these groups would find a thing. But the subsequent FBI

159

investigation would be more thorough and precautions had to be taken against it.

A lone man who had moved in shortly before the assassination—only to disappear immediately afterwards—was sure to arouse the curiosity of the FBI. So, his pad had to be safely removed from Elijah's crib.

His next act would be to buy a car. He planned to pay cash so the car he'd buy would be used. Anyone who purchased a new car with cash money attracted attention among the sales staff of a dealership. A black guy who did so would attract even more. Not too many brothers paid cash.

The third thing on his agenda was to arrange for surveillance of Elijah's mansion. He might need a way in or at least a way of finding out what was going on inside.

Tracey Bivens had taken a manuscript about contemporary jazz home with her. She did nearly all her reading at home.

With some amusement she noted that this writer, like many others these days, was obviously emulating Eric's style.

Where, by the way, was that knucklehead? He'd been away for months now and not a word had been heard from him. That was unlike Eric. Sure, he'd split at a moment's notice, but she would usually receive a letter or a least a card from him informing her that he was doing all right and where he could be reached.

Tomorrow she'd call his mother. Surely she'd know where he was.

Isaac Payne sat in his high-backed reading chair and prepared for his routine late night vigil. One of these nights, he was certain, his perseverance would pay off. Pisces would call his granddaughter. And when he did, the bug he'd had placed on her telephone would allow him to hear and record his every word. Hopefully he'd learn of the killer's location.

Patience, he told himself, was the key. He would eventually find Schofield and he would kill him. Not directly, of course. But he would orchestrate the assassin's demise. The future of the Nation of Islam depended upon it.

He was sure that there were many who'd been affected by Schofield's infamous deeds. Such people would more than likely be ecstatic over the opportunity to eliminate that international pest.

He, Ishaq Bayan, would merely have to locate such a person and provide him with a little guidance.

Schofield had found an apartment on Chicago's Westside and had settled in. The furnished apartment was in an above-average neighborhood where he could expect a degree of privacy that the Southside wouldn't provide.

He had also been surveilling Elijah's house and recording facts like the times the FOI security guard changed shifts and the identities of persons who most frequently were admitted into the mansion.

For a while Schofield had thought that he might kill one of the more frequent visitors, say one of the secretaries of the Temple, and disguise himself as her. But he had decided against such a tactic, considering it too risky.

But it had soon become clear to Eric what he had to do. There was but one day in the year that Elijah was sure to leave his home. That day was Saviour's Day, February 26. He would kill Elijah on that day.

He had no doubts about his ability to get a firearm past the FOI security at the General Richard L. Jones Armory where the conventions were normally held. But he was concerned about the escape after the hit.

He had thought about having a camera designed with a firing mechanism inside and posing as a photographer and killing Elijah while "photographing" him. But that would necessitate the hiring of someone to make such a device. Which also meant that he'd have to kill the maker soon after acquiring the gadget. For, once the manner of Elijah's death became known, the designer of the weapon would know that his weapon had been the instrument of death. It was possible that the maker of the weapon would talk to someone and from the flow of conversation, the police could be placed on Schofield's trail.

Then he thought of having a rifle made to resemble a cane. He would enter the convention as a blind man and pick the right time to blow Muhammad away.

Still too risky.

In the end Schofield decided that it would be best to kill Muhammad by sniper attack. He would hit Elijah in his car as he drove to the Armory to address the faithful at the Saviour's Day convention.

All he needed was the Messenger's planned travel route.

It had been two weeks since he'd hired Pete Fisher to investigate Isaac Payne. It was time to learn if his investment had been a prudent one.

He telephoned Fisher's office. Maria Perez answered.

"Peter Fisher, please."

"I'm sorry, Mr. Fisher's not in right now. May I help you?"

"Yes. You can tell me where I can contact him."

"Mr. Fisher's out of town, sir. I am not at liberty to give out his number. However, if you'll leave your..."

"My name is Bob Morgan."

"Oh! Mr. Morgan. Yes sir. I didn't know it was you. Pete, uh, Mr. Fisher left his number for you. He's in Boston." She stopped as if she expected Schofield to comment on this information.

"May I have the number, please?"

In Boston's redlight district Pete Fisher had picked up a

slender prostitute and escorted her to his hotel room. The prostitute, who was known as Pepper on the streets, had her head buried in Fisher's pubic hair.

"Yeah, bitch. Go for it," commanded Fisher huskily.

"Hot damn it!" he exclaimed. "Get me off. Get me off, bitch!"

The man's fat legs flopped about on the bed as the girl ministered to his urgent need. Feeling his climax mounting, Fisher raised his pink ass up off the bed.

"Oh Jesus! Shit!" Fisher screamed. His mammoth belly rippled with waves of blubber. The girl somehow managed to continue her task.

"Oh shit! Don't stop! I'm getting ready to come!"

Pepper reached under the slob's immense body to scratch his fat, pimply ass. For some reason, she had learned, a lot of fat guys dug that. So she did it for them. But there was no enthusiasm and no passion in her work.

It was strictly business

The whale-shaped hulk bucked mightily beneath her. She could feel the mounting tension in his shaft. She would be glad when it was all over.

Then the telephone rang.

The girl stopped and lifted her head.

"D-don't. . .don't stop now, stupid bitch!" Fisher was in agony.

"Come on," he said, trying to pull her head back to his groin.

"Shouldn't you get the phone?" asked the girl.

"Fuck the phone. Come on."

A puzzled look appeared on the girl's face. She shrugged slightly and returned to her ministrations. But Fisher's phallus had decreased considerably in hardness.

The phone rang on insistently. The girl's work became noticeably more mechanical. Fisher's erection was fast disappearing.

"Oh fuck it! Fuck it!"

Fisher picked up the phone.

"What!" he barked.

"I've been calling you, without success, all day," the voice said.

"Morgan? This Morgan?"

"Yes. I hope you have some information for me."

"Damn, Morgan. You pick a fine time...Sure. I got something for you. Wait a sec."

Fisher reluctantly slid out of bed and stomped across the room, his flesh jiggling with each step, and picked up a brown folder from his attache case.

"All right, Morgan. The guy you want..."

"Hold it!" Schofield interrupted. He nearly shouted.

"'Smatter?"

"You are not alone." It was a statement.

"Well, no. But, ah..."

"Get rid of her. Now!"

Shit. Twenty bucks down the fucking drain. But he knew Morgan was right.

"Hey," he said to Pepper. "Out. Get the fuck out." When she looked at him curiously but didn't move, he repeated, "Out, I said. I gotta talk. So scram."

Pepper, having received her gratuity in advance, was all too happy to split. Although she usually received tips for her labor, this time she didn't mind missing out on the bonus. She was happy enough just getting away from that creep.

In no time she was dressed and was gone.

"Okay, Morgan. I'm back."

When Schofield hung up he knew that he'd spent his money wisely. He didn't mind that the fat bastard was spending his nights fucking some whore—pity the poor girl who'd let *that* climb atop her—because his days were quite evidently being spent in superb investigatory work.

Isaac Payne, Fisher had told him, was known to hold card playing sessions with three other elderly men. The card sessions, though, were actually meetings. And Fisher had been able to find out the names of each participant. Each man lived in a different city.

But each had lived in Detroit, Michigan. During the same time period.

Each of the old men was filthy rich. One was an economist and financier, another was a psychologist, another a medical doctor and Payne himself was a lawyer.

While still in college and graduate school they had all been arrested together back in 1932. Then they had been released with all charges dropped.

There had been a hearing on police charges against one Wallace Fard aka Professor Ford. The four students had been charged, along with others, with creating a disturbance during the proceedings.

Fard was a man who, according to Detroit police records, had proclaimed himself "Supreme Ruler of the Universe."

Schofield knew he'd hit the jackpot. So pleased was he with the work Fisher had done, he didn't mind sending Fisher the extra money he'd requested. Supposedly he had to pay off a Detroit cop for digging up the data in the police archives.

Schofield was also happy because his study of the Nation of Islam's history was paying off.

Wallace Fard or Professor Ford was one of the many names used by Master Fard Muhammad, the Nation's founder, Elijah's teacher and the man the Muslims believed to be God in Person.

165

Chapter Fifteen

October, 1974

The two men were jogging slowly in Washington's Rock Creek Park. They pounded past the tennis court in the park's section that was called the Carter Baron. It was early morning and the sun had only recently risen over the eastern horizon.

While the older of the two ran smoothly and breathed rhythmically through his mouth, the younger man wasn't faring nearly as well.

"Why don't we stop a minute," huffed Roland Tyler. "I'm not ready for this." Before receiving a reply Tyler broke stride and reduced his speed to a slow walk. His breath came to him with extreme hardship.

"Did we have to meet out here?" Tyler asked. The early morning chill cut easily through Tyler's newly purchased sweatsuit. "Couldn't we talk in a restaurant or someplace warm like any other civilized people?"

Colonel Abraham Micah stared at Tyler scornfully.

"That is precisely why we're meeting here," sneered the Colonel. "Too many of your 'civilized' fellow bureaucrats are apt to stop off for a nice breakfast at one of your plush restaurants. How pampered you Americans are! And wouldn't we make an interesting pair? A Deputy Defense Secretary and an ex-MOSSAD agent conversing in the post-dawn morning? Conversing of what? I'm sure every politician in Washington would be dying to know." The Colonel took a deep breath, savoring the early morning freshness. "Tell me, Tyler. Are the other Pentagon big shots as woefully out of shape as you?"

"For a man asking for favors," said Tyler, "you sure have a caustic tongue." Tyler's breath was gradually becoming steadier.

"But the favors I am asking are not of you, but of your boss. Do not forget that. You are merely a message carrier. So please do not act as if I am requesting favors of *you*. You have nothing of value to offer. However, I do apologize if I have offended you. It just strikes me as odd that a leader in the Defense Department would strike such a defenseless posture. I should think such a thing detrimental to the morale of the fighting men."

A bicycle rider approached them on the trail and they stepped aside to allow her to pass.

"I have the names you want," said Tyler, tired of the colonel's sarcasm. "There are but ten blacks who are or were capable of carrying out the kinds of things you mentioned. I am referring to men who were active during the Vietnam war effort."

"Their names, please."

"Four of them are dead. You want those?"

"Of course not. Only the living ones." Now it was the Colonel's turn to become irritated.

"Two others were paralyzed. Perhaps you'd like a detailed biography of them. They were very tragically injured in the line of duty. Makes for exciting reading. Especially in view of the fact that one of them was aiding your beloved Israel."

"Mr. Tyler. I would appreciate..."

"Or take Oliver White. Now he's a real story. Driven mad by torture. Cambodians. Old Oliver slips into Phnom Penh, see, and..."

"Am I to understand that only three of the ten remain on an operational level?" asked Micah impatiently.

"Yep."

"Their names?" asked the Colonel again.

"David Thomas. Anthony Vick. Eric Schofield. Navy, CIA and Army Intelligence respectively."

They passed the amphitheatre.

"Okay. Tell me about them."

"Their prior activities or..."

"What they are up to now. I expect a full written report on their past assignments."

"Sure. You'll get that. Okay, Thomas is now a photographer. Quite successful, I might add. He takes pictures of those high fashion models and travels around the world snapping 'the beautiful people.' You know, the jet set."

"Have you a list of the dates and places of his travels?" Micah asked.

"Certainly. You'll have all that later today."

"And Vick?"

"A lot of foreign travel too. He owns a chain of exotic pet shops. He married into quite a bit of money. White wife. He likes to do much of the hunting and trapping himself. More of a hobby, I'd say, than anything else. He certainly doesn't need the money. He has some top notch people running his business while he's away. Which is pretty often."

168

"What about Schofield?"

"A writer."

"Travel much?"

"Not as frequently as the other two, but often enough. Two or three times a year. He's a music writer."

"He writes music?"

"No, he writes about music for magazines. Rock music. Has a couple of books out too.

"Of all the blacks to work in intelligence, Schofield seemed to have the most potential, till one day he just told his babysitter—his field supervisor—that he'd had it. Not so strange. A lot of guys get fed up. But they were so high on this guy. They figured to turn over a big piece of the African operation to him one day when he got too old for field action. That's what I hear, anyway.

"Everybody and his momma tried to convince the guy to stay on. But he was adamant."

"What reason did he give for quitting?"

"Said he was tired of killing people. Hey! It happens all the time. One day a tiger, next day a rabbit. What can we do? He simply didn't re-enlist."

"You do keep a check on your people, don't you? The ones who retire, I mean."

Tyler thought for a moment. Then he said, "Frankly, that's one of the things that's bothering me. They are supposed to be called in on a regular basis and full reports—detailed reports—should be compiled annually. But everybody's been just sort of going through the motions the past few years. Vietnam. The oil crisis. Watergate. I don't know. Our problems, right? Anyway, the answer is no. There hasn't been enough checkup. No one seems to care. As long as they don't run to the media or write books about their experiences or blow any covers, who gives a damn?

"But Christ! These guys are lethal! You got all kinds of

retirees, black and white, walking around and any one of them could fuck up an entire city!

"Take the three guys we're talking about. What if they joined an underground guerrilla group? Or the Black Panthers or something? Whoosh!" He spread his hands in a gesture meant to represent an explosion.

Eric Schofield felt like he knew the Southside of Chicago like his own neighborhood. He'd been up and down Cottage Grove, Stoney Island and all the major streets and back alleyways so many times that he knew every building.

Finding a suitable place from which to shoot Elijah Muhammad wouldn't pose a problem. Such places are numerous.

All that remained was for him to find out what route the aging Messenger planned to take.

Chapter Sixteen

November, 1974

Sleep refused to come to Marsha Payne. For several weeks her days had been filled with worry over the man she knew as Kevin Stone. Her nights were filled with dreams of the man she longed for. Her mornings brought her anguish and disappointment because her awakenings were accomplished alone.

Of late, though, she had found that her concern over Kevin's well-being was being mixed with another emotion. Anger. She had begun to consider herself foolish to have thought that Kevin really cared, that he felt as she did. Their time together had been so short, she was certain that she'd blown things way out of proportion.

She must have afforded him a real good laugh. But now she was almost ready to face it. She had been, as far as he was concerned, merely an easy lay. And that made her angry.

But she remembered the first night that he said he loved her. His voice had been filled with such sincerity when he spoke the words.

How could he have lied? Perhaps she was jumping to conclusions. He did say that he would be gone for a good while and that he might be unable to get in touch for months. He'd asked her to have faith, to not doubt that he loved her and he would come back. But how long can one maintain faith?

Despite her anger she had to admit to herself that she still loved him as much as she ever did. Only now some of her love, instead of being expressed in passion, was manifesting itself in feelings of anger born of neglect.

She got out of bed—she couldn't sleep anyway—and walked into her small kitchen. She opened up the refrigerator and brought out a pint of yogurt. She hadn't eaten dinner and it had dawned upon her that she was hungry.

She went into the living room and placed a record on the stereo. She sat on her loveseat and picked at her yogurt while the album by the Fifth Dimension played.

She got up to pick up an issue of *Scientific American* that she had neglected to read. Since she was going to be up, she thought, she might as well do something constructive. She decided that science was the farthest thing from her mind and that she would never be able to concentrate on the scholarly pieces in *Scientific American*.

So she would just sit there, feel sorry for herself, and eat her yogurt. She thought of that old song that said "It's my party and I'll cry if I want to." She had a right, she felt, to feel sorry for herself.

So involved was she with her own blue mood that she barely heard the telephone ringing. When it dawned upon her three rings had already sounded, she finally lifted the receiver.

"Marsha."

"Kevin!" She could hardly believe it. "Is this Kevin?"

"Well, at least you remember my name."

Simultaneous with the ringing of Marsha's phone, an alarm sounded in the Boston apartment of her grandfather, Isaac Payne.

Payne was only able to personally catch the tail end of the conversation. But the recording device which was attached to the apparatus caught every word. He heard his granddaughter ask, "Are you outside, darling? You sound cold."

"Yeah," he heard Schofield reply. "I'm at a pay phone. It's cold as hell."

Payne realized that he wouldn't be able to pinpoint Schofield's exact location, as long as he utilized pay phones. But he would be able to get a general idea of Schofield's location by learning the area from which he made his calls to Marsha. He estimated that it would take about five more calls before he could make an educated guess as to where Schofield's base of operations was.

He heard Schofield sign off: "Love you babes. For real." His granddaughter returned the endearments.

He didn't like the fact that he had been the cause of his Marsha falling in love with a murderer.

Colonel Abraham Micah looked up at the apartment building on Riverside Drive. In a minute he'd go in, but he wasn't quite ready yet. He hiked up his collar against the autumn wind. He disliked the cold and he wasn't used to such weather anymore.

He had visited Anthony Vick and David Thomas posing as a newspaper reporter. Both of them were eager to talk. But, as he expected, neither had anything interesting to say. At least not interesting to him. But then, neither of them had

173

been out of the country on January 20, 1973. Still he had to make sure.

Eric Schofield, however, had been abroad on that day. That was the day. That was the day Amicar Cabral had been killed. And while Micah didn't give a damn about a dead African, he knew that whoever had killed Cabral had also killed Ambassador Yacob.

Tracey Bivens sat on her living room sofa and read the science fiction manuscript that her boss at Snoden Associates had asked her to check out. Sci-fi wasn't her bag, but there was a very big market for it. Snoden Associates had only recently decided to get a piece of the action.

Okay, she thought. No problem. Just don't overload me with this crap. But, she conceded, the manuscript she had wasn't really all that bad. In fact, she was actually enjoying it.

An obscure Milwaukee inventor has devised a method of travel in outer space via teleportation. He bumps into every kind of monster imaginable and, finally, reaches a planet of honest to goodness mermaids. He falls in love with one of them and...and where the hell was that damn Eric Schofield?

He'd been away for months. And she hadn't heard a word from him. Where in Europe had he gone? She felt now that she should have pressured him into being more specific about his destination.

She went back to the book. Now the space traveler and his mermaid were encountering a very fundamental obstacle to the longevity of their lovelife. She breathed water and he breathed air. Wow! Was this writer serious? She was glad she and Eric at least both breathed air.

The doorbell broke her reverie.

Tracey jumped at the sound. Who could that possibly be? Nobody was supposed to get upstairs without the doorman's permission. And then the only way he would give permission was if she approved the visitor for entry.

Perhaps it was a neighbor, one of the building residents. However, as it was past eleven o'clock, she doubted that her neighbors—none of whom were more than casual acquaintances—would be visiting.

Tracey raced into her bedroom to don a bathrobe. She slid her feet into her slippers and returned to the living room to answer the door.

"Who's there?" she asked tentatively.

"It's the police. May be come in, Miss Bivens?"

Instinctively she moved to release the police lock on the door. Even as she was lifting the bar it occurred to her that she should have asked to see some identification before admitting the man or men outside.

But it was too late now because the lock had been lifted and two men were in the process of entering her apartment. Both men were large, over six feet. Both were white. One was in his late fifties and the other in his twenties. They were not in uniform, but they wore the kind of drab, cheap business suits all New York detectives seemed to crave.

"We're here to ask you about Eric Schofield," said the older man gravely.

"Oh my goodness! Something has happened to Eric?"

"No, not at all," said Colonel Abraham Micah. "Do you know where we can reach him?"

"He left the...uh, no. I don't know." There was something strange, something unsettling about his pair. Suddenly, she was afraid to give them any information about Schofield.

She's lying, thought Martin Kahn. His eyes expressed the thought to Micah.

"Perhaps we should explain," said Micah paternally. I'm Detective Robert Strother. This is my partner, John Barker."

175

"Do you, uh, mind showing me some identification?" asked Tracey.

Tracey watched their faces closely. The older man hardly reacted at all, as if the request for I.D. was something he encountered daily. But the younger man's face tightened and his pupils seemed to dilate.

"Sure, ma'am," he answered too accommodatingly.

The older man reached for his wallet, obviously confident, thought Tracey, that his identification would be convincing. But the younger man already had his out and displayed a card with the N.Y.P.D. lettering and symbol. His own photo graced the plastic card.

When the older man offered his to Tracey, she said, "That's okay. I'm sure you're cops."

She wasn't sure of anything of the kind.

"Mr. Schofield," began Colonel Micah, "left this address with us. I was told that he could be contacted here. You see, the Mayor is going to have a dinner in honor of the contributions of black music to American culture. As a leading authority on that genre, Mr. Schofield is, of course, invited and urged to attend."

If that's the case, Tracey wondered, why send cops? Why not just send an invitation. And why come at eleven o'clock?

As if reading her thoughts Colonel Micah said: "Of course, we have to screen all prospective visitors to Gracie Mansion. Irksome, but necessary. Security." He waved his hand as though dismissing the ridiculous ritual.

"We were unable," Micah continued, "to catch him at his apartment in Sharon Hill, Pennsylvania. So we thought that he might be here. We wanted to wrap this up this evening, so please forgive our arriving at this hour. We would have called, but your number's not listed."

"I see." It occurred to Tracey that this so-called cop was doing an awful lot of explaining for a New York cop talking

176

to a black woman. City police treated black people like rat turds, so why was this fellow so polite and informative?

Tracey felt her stomach jerk. She was honestly afraid of these men. They seemed very sinister, so capable of cruelty.

"Give me your number. And if Eric calls or comes back..."

"Just have him call the Twenty-Eighth District. Ask for me. By the way, when's the last time you talked with Mr. Schofield?"

"About a week ago," Tracey lied. She didn't know why, but she felt the worst thing she could do was to give these men a single correct fact.

The two men thanked her for her time, apologized again for the hour, and departed.

Tracey breathed a sigh of relief. Then goose pimples broke out on her back and arms.

Those men couldn't have been New York cops. They had foreign accents.

Chapter Seventeen

The Fruit of Islam security guards were assigned to guard Muhammad's Temple of Islam No. 2 around the clock.

Temple No. 2 of the Holy Temple of Islam was the headquarters of the Nation of Islam. All administrative directives to the various regions issued from this huge edifice located at 7351 South Stoney Island Avenue in Chicago.

The building had originally been a Greek Orthodox Church. It had been purchased by the Honorable Elijah Muhammad's followers with the money from a loan from Libya's Colonel Mu'amman El-Qathafi. The purchase price was four million dollars. The Temple housed the offices of the Supreme Captain of the FOI, the National Secretary and the Minister of the Temple and the Mid-West Regional Minister, who was also the assistant of the Messenger of Allah.

The only Muslim sanctuary more zealously guarded was

the Apostle's own mansion.

FOI soldiers were posted at the door and had a full view of the courtyard as well as much of Stoney Island Avenue. Other soldiers were stationed outside in an automobile. Still more periodically patrolled the Temple's grounds. They communicated via walkie-talkie.

As the Chicago Muslims were both feared and respected, the FOI on security seldom saw any action. Those with grievances against the Muslims were rarely foolish enough to vent their displeasure in acts of vandalism.

The Muslims had, however, compiled an impressive record of violence. Some of it had been perpetrated against the Messenger's followers. On one occasion the Supreme Captain had been wounded by an unknown sniper a few years ago. A minister had been shot by one of the teachers at the University of Islam. The teacher, a Muslim, was said to be crazed. One of the Temple captains was murdered in the assault.

There were good reasons for the tight security. And the FOI remained vigilant on their posts. Random surprise visits, spot checks, from lieutenants and occasionally the Supreme Captain himself, kept the Fruit on constant battle alert.

But the focal point of the Temple security was the prevention of entry from without. Very little—except for a very casual check—was done to secure the Temple from within.

Eric Schofield capitalized on this deficiency in the system. In fact, Schofield was unimpressed with the entire arrangement. Rank amateurism, in his opinion. He conceded that it was probably sufficient for scaring off angry blacks or racist whites. But it was as nothing against a trained professional.

Schofield emerged from the closet in the office of the captain of the female unit, the M.G.T.G.C.C. (Muslim Girls

Training and General Civilization Class).

Having learned that the FOI were expressly forbidden by the Messenger from "meddling in the affairs" of the M.G.T., Schofield was certain that the FOI soldiers would, if they checked at all, only glance inside the office of the M.G.T. captain.

When they made their regular post-meeting check, they completely bypassed the M.G.T. captain's office.

When the Wednesday night meeting of the Temple commenced Eric Schofield was in attendance. Arriving promptly at eight o'clock, clean shaven, hair closely cropped and sporting a large bow tie, he sat down in the back rows with the FOI members. Visitors sat towards the front.

In a smaller Temple he couldn't have pulled it off. Everybody knew everyone else. But in the huge Temple where there were so many believers, it was possible. The turnover was so rapid that no one was sure who was a registered Muslim and who wasn't. Even the lieutenants and squad leaders had a hard time keeping up with the full registry. But they didn't like to ask because it gave the appearance of incompetence. A lieutenant who couldn't identify his troops? Unheard of. Yet there were so many new believers "accepting their own" that a scorecard was needed to keep track of all of them.

Schofield wore a dark blue, conservative suit. He generously applied cocoa butter to his face to give him the much-ballyhooed facial shine that supposedly represented spirituality and cleanliness.

He was a bona fide Muslim. He even sat, as did many others, with both hands resting atop his right knee, a standard FOI sitting posture.

He had waited until the meeting was going strong, until the minister was "smoking." As the minister heated up his sermon with calls for God to "destroy this blond-haired, blue-eyed devil," the faithful followers heated up their shouting (euphemistically called witness bearing).

"I know some of you don't like to hear us tell you the truth," the minister preached.

"That's right!" responded the followers.

"But I have to tell the truth."

"Teach brother!"

"Do you want to hear the truth?"

"Yes sir! Yes sir!"

"Oh no you don't! That's the problem with the black man. He don't want to hear the truth!"

"Expose 'em, Brother Minister! Expose 'em!"

"What is the truth?"

"Good question!"

"The truth is that Allah is God!"

"Go 'head, Brother."

"The white man is the devil!"

"Burn that devil."

"The Honorable Elijah Muhammad is the Messenger of Allah in your very midst!"

"Come on!"

"And you have a choice!"

"Make it plain!"

"To accept Islam and live . . ."

"Break it down! Break it down!"

"Or reject Islam . . ."

"Teach, Brother! Teach!"

"And die!"

"Yes! Yes! Teach! Make it plain, Brother Minister!"

The auditorium exploded with the applause of the audience. Eric Schofield selected this moment of religious euphoria to slip out of his seat and ease back to the area of the Temple where the offices were situated.

Everybody, even the money-conscious secretaries, were enraptured by the minister's fiery preaching. It was not that he was saying anything new, but he shouted out the dogma with such force and conviction that everyone was moved. No one paid Schofield any attention when he slipped into a restroom. Nor was he observed taking a metal pick from the refill of his ink pen. (The search post soldier checked his pen by clicking it while pointing it at him. But no one thought to look inside the refill itself.)

When he slipped the pick inside the door's lock he heard the minister. The tempo had slowed now. He was more subdued.

"Tonight I want to introduce you to a man! A man who has suffered more hardships than you can imagine! A man who stood up for black people before it was popular to even call yourself black! A man who said, at a time that nobody else wanted you, 'I want them. I want to put the black man on top!'

"A man who defends you, who works day and night for you! Who cannot rest, who will not rest, until each and every one of you is free!

"Yes, tonight I'd like to introduce you to a man! You obviously don't know him because to know him is to love him. So allow me to introduce you to a man, the man, that the very souls of the so-called American Negroes have cried out for, for ages! Cried out for solace, cried out for comfort, for guidance, for defense!

"Let me present to you," he held high a photograph of the Messenger, "the only black leader in America! The Most Honorable Elijah Muhammad!"

In the explosive applause that followed the Minister's remarks, the sharp clicking sound made by Schofield's opening of the lock went unheard.

Eric Schofield settled himself comfortably on the floor of

the closet. He could sit motionless for four or five hours. In Vietnam he had to be prepared to lay motionless, when encircled by the enemy, for a full day or longer if need be.

Hours had passed and Schofield looked at his watch, luminous in the closet's darkness. It was one o'clock in the morning. The Temple was nearly empty, Schofield could tell, from the scarcity of sounds.

The outside patrolman had come inside the Temple to catch the warmth. Schofield could hear him talking to the FOI who were stationed at the door.

The doorman was apparently newly married. He was worried about how his wife was reacting to his first night away from home. He didn't really want to be there, but as it was his turn for night duty, what could he say?

The outside patrolman was a bachelor. He just hoped his relief man would arrive at 6:00 A.M. He had to go to work in the morning. If the relief arrived on time, he'd be able to go home, shower, shave and take the bus to the Loop where he worked.

Schofield emerged from the closet. He didn't expect the information he sought to be in the M.G.T. captain's office. What he wanted was, if he had guessed the FOI hierarchy's thinking correctly, a security matter. And security fell under the domain of the Supreme Captain.

From the sounds of their conversation, Schofield placed the Fruit at the front door of the Temple.

He peeked out of the office. There was no one in sight. He walked out and over to the Supreme Captain's office. He inserted his pick inside the lock. Carefully, he wriggled it.

Click.

"Did you hear something?" asked the doorman.

"Naw. Just the wind, if anything. Yeah, so I told the brother, I said, 'Look brother. I don't know who you think you are...'"

183

Schofield was glad, very glad, that the FOI hadn't investigated the sound he had made. Two dead FOI would cause excessive security arrangements, making his job considerably more difficult.

Schofield went straight to the file cabinets. He went through several drawers. Nothing. Finally, he opened a drawer marked personnel. He found folders marked: "Bakery," "Cleaners," "Clothing Store," "Bank," and "Messenger's House."

Jackpot!

He had a choice. He could either photocopy the pages in the folder marked "Messenger's House" or he could relax and study the dossiers there in the office.

If he copied the pages he could go home and read them at his leisure. If he did so, though, he ran the risk of alerting the Fruit to his presence. The Xerox just might be one of those noisy jobs.

He couldn't take the risk. So, for the next three hours he made himself at home in the Supreme Captain's office.

Actually, it was a very nice office. Soft carpet. Stylish furniture. If only he had a cigarette. But then he wouldn't want to desecrate a holy house, would he?

The words "holy house," for some reason, caused him to recall that Elijah Muhammad had once said that his own Temple No. 2 was "honey-combed with hypocrites." Some holy house. Too bad he didn't have any cigarettes.

Each folder on the employees at The House included a snapshot and biographical profile of the person. Also observations of the person's strengths and weaknesses were made.

Schofield thought that the dossiers were in no way comparable to the professional quality he'd seen the Army compile, but he still felt a tinge of pride that unprofessional blacks could produce anything approaching the quality he beheld.

After a while Schofield narrowed his possible selection to two women secretaries. He pondered over the choice for another hour.

Finally, his eyes heavy with fatigue, he chose his unwitting assistant in the murder of Elijah Muhammad.

Her name was Gwendolyn Akbar.

Eric Schofield had exited Muhammad's Temple No. 2 via a window in the Supreme Captain's office. He walked to his car which was parked two blocks away.

Now, in his apartment, Schofield's mood became melancholy. He removed his clothing and lay in bed. But sleep wouldn't come, despite the fact he was dog tired. The events of the day and the events to come refused to allow rest.

His thoughts raced back over the years. To Vietnam. To the jungles there and to the fat and pampered American-supported puppets in Saigon. Puppets he'd worked with, protected, transported, and when so ordered, killed. A strange time. A strange land. A strange, strange war.

His thoughts carried him to Africa and the confusing tribal and national conflicts that were exploited by big business and foreign government.

Back to America and Laura came the thoughts that played against his inner forehead like a motion picture. It was a motion picture which, having begun, he was powerless to shut off. He saw himself and Laura in bed, laughing at an old late-night movie.

She, who never wasted words, had found the need to speak. Her voice still rang in his ears. I love you, Eric. I always will. He could count the times she had said those words. She didn't say it often, but he knew that she did. He remembered thinking her saying it then was peculiar.

Now, in the mental picture, Laura smiled weakly, touching

185

her stomach. Her belly leapt, a muscle spasm curling in her small stomach the size of a softball.

He saw his own eyes widen in confusion.

She reached for him.

Then the blood came. Rivers of gushing blood.

He snatched back the covers. She squeezed him, crushing his breath.

Oh Eric! I'm sorry!

He placed his hands over her vagina, vainly trying to stop the torrent of blood. So much blood.

Eric forgive me, please! A boy, Eric. A little boy!

And the blood rushed past his fingers. He then saw himself, totally naked, snatching her up and rushing off to the hospital.

The movie slowed down. He saw himself bursting into the emergency ward, naked and crazed, carrying a package he knew was already dead.

Sleep still evaded him although he was exhausted.

The movie continued to play inside his now aching head.

He saw himself reading Laura's diary. He recalled the weeks of walking about in a stupor, empty and emaciated. He had been bewildered. He didn't know why she had done it. Until he read the diary.

For me. She did it for me and my shitty assed career.

He recalled his failure to meet the deadlines for the articles he had been assigned to write. He recalled the irate editors.

His memory reproduced the ad in *Soldier of Fortune* magazine calling for mercenaries to earn big money in Africa. Eric found himself in Africa once again. And he found Musa Ibn Mahmoud. Or had Musa found him? He had never been quite sure.

The fat little Arab fitted incongruously with the black Africans. Because Eric spoke Arabic, the Arab was attracted to him.

"I've read your record of wartime experiences," the Arab

186

had said. "I am familiar with the kind of training you underwent. What, in God's name, are you doing among this band of crude mercenaries? These men are not in your class at all. Do you want to make some money? I mean real money?"

Mahmoud knew Schofield by the name of Robert Jennings. It was a false name and Mahmoud knew that without asking. But he was accustomed to such practices.

Eric had also supplied him with phony dates and assignments which the Arab probably knew were equally false. But the experiences were real. He had done things like the things he had reported. And the Arab was aware of this too.

These reminiscences were interspersed with Laura's cry that fatal night: A boy, Eric! A little boy!

"With your talents," the Arab was saying, "you'd never have to worry about money again. People will pay dearly for your service."

Laura had written in the diary: "Eric just can't afford a child. It would ruin his career. Oh God! I want this child so badly. But..."

Ibn Mahmoud had been right. He did need to make some real money. He never intended to have to worry about money again.

The faces of some of his victims rolled past his mind. For most he felt nothing. For some he felt some small satisfaction. They had been well deserving of death and he would gladly kill them again. For a very few he felt sorrow. For Amicar Cabral he felt grief. This one might have united all of Africa one day.

Real money. How do you make the money to pay for all this? His friends often asked him after his career as an assassin had proven most lucrative. He soon came to realize that he badly needed a cover. He needed an answer to the

187

"what do you do for a living" question. He dusted off his old typewriter. He became a writer again. He unearthed his "career." Laura would have been ecstatic. He dedicated this labor to her. It was, in truth, a labor of love.

Then his mind played back scenes that featured Tracey, and his heart was warmed by thoughts of her.

But mental pictures of Marsha soon pushed those of Tracey from his mind and he realized that he did love her. He loved her differently from Tracey. It was a different and more dangerous love.

How many chicks can one dude love simultaneously?

He thought of the fact that some Arabs had as many as four wives. His tired lips smiled. Maybe them A-rabs know something we don't.

The next picture that appeared on the screen of his mind was that of a man. A not-yet-dead man. Elijah Muhammad.

Eric suddenly felt very sad. Inexplicably, he felt devoid of purpose. What was all this for, anyway? Was it really for the money? If so, he certainly didn't need the money now. The "career" Laura had so nobly and needlessly died for was now paying him more than he would ever spend.

So why didn't he stop? Was it revenge for his loss of Laura? Or was it sadism? Sport? Did he kill people for sport? The old man had suggested that he needed a challenge. Was that true?

Maybe this would be it. Maybe this would close out that phase of his life. Maybe he would kill no more. Maybe.

But first there was the unfinished business. Elijah.

He pulled his nude body from the bed. Sleep teased him but he remained adamantly opposed to satisfying his craving. He pulled his clothing over his lithe body. It was November and it was cold. He walked out, embracing the biting chill, becoming a part of it. When he estimated that he'd walked more than a mile, he stepped inside a telephone booth.

Isaac Payne's alarm rang simultaneously with Marsha Payne's telephone. Payne wouldn't awaken for this call but the recorder would pick up every word. He'd found it impossible to listen to her every call unless he taped them and listened to them at his leisure.

Most of Marsha's calls were from school chums who spoke endlessly of fashions, school events, boys or young men and, quite infrequently, of academic matters.

He would listen to the calls tomorrow. He would later discover that the one from Schofield—the fifth he'd made—fell within the one mile perimeter that had been marked to indicate Schofield's other calls.

Isaac Payne would look at his map of Chicago and the thick red square he'd drawn around one square mile of the Windy City's real estate. Inside that square lived Eric Schofield. Of this the old man was sure.

When sleep finally came to Eric Schofield the last thoughts that his mind entertained were of Gwendolyn Akbar. Already he had formulated a plan for meeting her.

Chapter Eighteen

December, 1974

Carol Spring pressed the phone against her ear and meticulously filed her nails. After a year of marriage the former Carol Clarke still experienced heart flutters when she talked to her husband, even on the phone.

Nathan Spring had been considered a prize catch. And she thanked God or fate or Lady Luck that she happened into his life at just the right time.

Some women would've had misgivings over marrying a man who had just come off a heart-breaking split with his woman of several years. But that didn't bother Carol one iota. The pain Nathan had experienced set the stage for him to recognize just how much she, Carol, had to offer.

She didn't feel as though she was getting a hand-me-down husband. She was simply happy that she and Nathan had gotten together. She didn't even have bad feelings toward

Nathan's former girl friend. How could she? By her neglect of Nathan for her career, she'd chased the man into her, Carol's, arms. Thank you, Tracey Bivens. Your loss is my gain.

And Nathan, she knew, was happier now. He once said: "I'm glad Tracey wouldn't marry me now. I'm glad I was free when I met you."

She believed him. The unshakable rule of their marriage was: "No bullshit. . .under any circumstances." They spoke straight talk to each other.

"Do you ever fantasize about making love, you know, to guys you were with in the past?"

"Yes," she replied, immediately fearful of the repercussions.

"Me too," he had said.

They'd found that they could discuss the most personal of subjects, and that they were free of many of the jealousies that plagued most marriages. They were secure with and in each other and, consequently, no external persons posed a threat to them.

"Honey, you know I don't ask you this often," Carol was saying into the phone.

"I'm not a chauvinist," Nathan's voice replied over the phone, "but there are limits. Next you'll be having me nurse the baby."

"We don't have a baby," Carol laughed.

"Not for lack of trying, m'dear. Not for lack of the old collegiate endeavor," said Nathan.

Carol Spring was Roland Tyler's secretary. Her office was at the Pentagon. Her husband was talking from his office, Caldwell, Belgrave and Spring, where he was a junior partner in the law firm. Almost daily they telephoned each other to break up their business day.

"You be a good boy and do like I ask and we can try again

tonight," Carol teased.

"Oh gee," mocked Nathan. "Are ya really gonna do it? Are ya gonna let me git a li'l bit o' dat sweet poontang of yoursen?"

"Oh, go to hell, Natie." She laughed aloud. "Come on now, are you going to do it? Please?"

"All right. God! But don't tell anybody. It doesn't fit my macho reputation, you know what I mean?"

When they'd hung up, Patricia Williams, another Pentagon secretary, asked about the conversation.

"Oh, I had to twist his arm to get him to cook dinner tonight. Some friends are coming over and I just have to do some shopping. Can't put it off. So I had to ask Natie to cook."

"Boy! You sure have it good. Billy never cooks for me," Pat said. "How'd you do it?"

Carol looked about and then whispered conspiratorially: "I promised him some pussy." Carol enjoyed embarrassing people with her raunchy talk.

"Oh, get out of here," said Pat, laughing and waving Carol off with her hand. "You're a sex pervert."

"Hey, are those plumbers still fixing the john?" Carol asked.

"One doesn't refer to the ladies room as a john," said Pat.

"The jane then. Whatever you call it, I gotta go."

"Nope," said Pat. "They won't be finished until tomorrow. Better use the one upstairs."

"Shit. Why should I walk that flight of stairs when I can use old Droopy Drawers' toilet? He's not in. Later for his stupid rules."

"Old Droopy Drawers" was the name the secretaries had secretly bestowed upon their boss, Deputy Defense Secretary Roland Tyler. One of the girls had engaged in a bit of after-office acrobatics with Tyler and Tyler had showed up for

192

the occasion wearing polka-dotted underwear which sagged badly in the seat.

When the girl informed her friends, Tyler was forevermore christened "Droopy Drawers" in inner-office gossip.

"Go ahead and use his bathroom," Pat said. "But if Droops catches you, you're on your own."

Tyler's private bathroom was a symbol of his prestige. He guarded it jealously and forbade his secretaries from using his precious possession. It took a daring act for a secretary to, in defiance of his command, plop her butt atop his stool.

Carol, today, felt daring. She dashed into the boss's office and stepped gingerly into his private washroom.

She made herself comfortable and admired the luxury that surrounded her. Her thoughts drifted to her shopping plans and the night's dinner party.

It was a nice bathroom, stylishly designed and comfortable. Not at all harsh and impersonal like the public rooms the secretaries had to use.

And no sooner had she gotten over the initial jitters of being in forbidden territory, than who should barge into the office but Roland Tyler.

Pat Williams giggled uncontrollably at Carol's predicament. Boy! Carol's gonna shit when she hears Droopy Drawers' voice. Then she remembered that she was already shitting. That thought made her laugh so hard that her belly ached.

Carol had indeed heard Tyler storm into the office and slam shut the door. She froze on the toilet stool, not knowing what to do. He would hit the ceiling if he saw her coming out of his bathroom.

She sat silently, scared to move from the stool. She heard him bumping into things in the office, taking down books, pulling open drawers only to slam them shut immediately. Then she heard him place something heavier than a book on the desktop.

She heard a clicking sound. The dictaphone. Tyler had long been in the habit of taping his daily activities for the memoirs he was sure he'd write when his time in government expired after a long and, he hoped, prosperous career.

The tapings, which Tyler took most seriously, were a very private matter to him. Nobody was allowed to be present during these sessions and, in the aftermath of Watergate, he didn't really want anyone to know he was doing them.

But, of course, Carol knew. She was, like it or not, one of his secretaries.

"December 9, 1974," she heard his nasal voice say. "I met with Colonel Abraham Micah as arranged in Central Park. As suspected, he is operating independent of MOSSAD. He and others, numbers unknown, all former MOSSAD agents, are hunting down a Negro assassin.

Carol wanted to flush herself down the toilet. I shouldn't be hearing this. All of it is probably classified. But to allow her presence to be known now would be disastrous. He might even fire her.

"Micah met with me a month ago. At that time I gave him three names of possible black American assassins. They were Anthony Vick, Eric Schofield and David Thomas."

She was most uncomfortable on that toilet. Please God, get me out of this. Hey! One of those names sounds familiar!

"Micah now is certain that the man he's after is Eric Schofield, ex-Army intelligence man. It is likely, even probable, that Micah intends to terminate Schofield. I have decided not to report this, at this time.

Carol was stunned. She knew she'd heard that name somewhere before. But where? It wasn't like she'd read his name in the papers. No, she knew this guy. Or she knew somebody who knew him. *". . .that Micah intends to terminate Schofield."* Carol was astonished.

Click. Tyler had turned off the dictaphone. She heard the door swing open and shut. "Where the hell's Carol?" she heard him whine.

"Upstairs," came Pat's voice. "In the ladies room, I think."

Thanks a lot, Pat.

"Well, I'm going downstairs. Ring His Majesty. Let him know I'm on my way."

"His Majesty" was the way the Deputy Secretary referred to his boss, the Secretary of Defense. Everybody had a nickname for everybody else, it seemed to Pat.

He left.

Flush.

Carol hurried from the bathroom and out of the office. She was shaking like a leaf.

Maurice and Allison Forrest laughed heartily at another of Nathan Spring's jokes. As always, they were enjoying themselves on this evening at the Springs'.

Nathan was the never-tiring life of the party. He assumed the role of entertainer and he wore the role comfortably. As usual, Carol turned down her own burners to play a supporting role to Nathan's center stage antics. When her husband was going strong she played the pouting, mildly offended, astonished and embarrassed perfect wife who tolerated her barely civilized spouse. But her efforts to tame her wild lover were accompanied by pleasant smiles that actually only served to spur him on all the more.

But, this night, Carol—for all practical purposes—wasn't even there. The girl was obviously out of it. She had tried gallantly to make her contributions to the gaiety of the night, but her attention, her thoughts, were quite evidently elsewhere. She had been caught, more than once, staring blankly when someone was addressing her.

"Oh, I'm sorry, what was that you just said?" she had stated on more than one occasion.

Yet Maurice and Nathan were having such fun that they hadn't noticed that something was troubling Carol. Troubling her deeply.

"Hon, would you get us some more vodka?" asked Nathan between jokes.

Carol walked stiffly to the bar to refill their glasses. No one seemed to notice when she kept pouring the clear liquid past the full point, spilling it on the counter top. Allison had noticed though, and walked over to her.

"What's wrong, dear? You look terrible."

"Oh, I'm terribly sorry, Allie. I just..."

"That's about the fifth time you've apologized tonight. Please tell me what's bothering you. You're not yourself, Carol, and you can't fool me."

"It's really nothing, Allie. Nothing serious."

"You don't want to talk, right?"

"Let me see if I can handle it. If I can't, I'll talk it over with you," Carol said.

"Promise?"

"Promise."

"Then I'll collect my slightly inebriated hubby and we'll be gone. Thanks for a lovely dinner. Or should I thank Nate?"

"Yeah," Carol smiled weakly. "Nate could always cook circles around me."

"Please don't hesitate to call me, if I can help. I mean that."

"Okay."

The Forrests had departed, and Nathan, not yet down from his on-stage high, helped Carol straighten up.

She was still shook up from the experience she'd had in the office earlier in the day. "...*intends to terminate*

Schofield.'' Sure, she'd heard things, read things, and knew that the Pentagon was rumored to be into clandestine domestic activities. But she never took that kind of talk too seriously. To her, the Pentagon was just the place she worked. All they did in her office was paperwork. Records. Statistics. Memos. But this was incredible. Yet Tyler, she knew, had been coldly serious.

Somehow, she was certain, this Eric Schofield had something to do with her household. Her maternal instincts reacted adversely to the idea, as though she and hers were being threatened by the planned elimination of this person.

"Darling, does the name Eric Schofield mean anything to you?" she asked at last.

Nathan's face tightened. He squinted his eyes. And before he even answered, Carol remembered who Eric Schofield was. She was sorry, then, that she'd brought his name up to her husband.

Schofield was the focal point of Tracey Bivens' career. And that very career was the thing that had stopped Nathan and Tracey from marrying.

Now those omniscient gossip columnists were calling Schofield and Tracey "an item."

Nathan was in love with his wife—Carol was secure in that knowledge—but she was realistic enough to know that the kind of feeling he'd had for Tracey wouldn't vanish overnight. There was some love left for Tracey and she accepted that.

Martin Kahn was a neophyte. He was in it for adventure and because of a romantic notion that he, alone, could be a great defender of the State of Israel. Micah, right now, had to use Kahn, and Kahn would be rewarded for his service. But the young man really had no future in espionage.

To launch the manhunt for Pisces, human resources and

197

connections beyond Micah's own power were required. It was for this reason that he found himself waiting in the lobby of the Jewish Defense League.

His appointment with Rabbi Milton Steinberg was long overdue. Quite obviously the fanatical JDL leader was making an exhibition of the scope and volume of his responsibilities. So busy was he that he had to keep an ex-MOSSAD officer waiting.

Micah had always found such posturing disgusting. They were in a time of extreme duress and so many Jews wasted time with stupid appearances. So much like the contemptible goyim.

It was two o'clock. The appointment with Steinberg had been for one-thirty. Micah quietly fumed.

No doubt the publicity-hungry JDL leader would blab to the press about how MOSSAD itself had come for JDL assistance, hoping to boost his own credibility by the fact. But there was no other way. Like it or not, Steinberg had the manpower and—it reflected the sordid state of things—there was a place in the Zionist thrust for people like him. Maybe even, in the final analysis, a fanatic like him was the best Jew of all.

The wooden door of the storefront flew open and the relentless winter wind rushed in. Behind the wind, a fat man bounced in wearing a checkered coat and stingy-brimmed hat. The fat man's pants legs were so short, the beginnings of his pink calves could be seen. Colonel Micah looked up and beheld Peter Fisher.

For the first time in days the Colonel smiled.

"Hi ya, hi ya!" Fisher greeted all and sundry. "I'm here to see the Rabbi."

A young secretary told Fisher to take a seat next to Micah. "You're after the gentleman there," she said pointing at the Colonel.

"He's *before* me?" Fisher was incredulous. "Honey, what I got can't wait! I'm here to help you all, you betcha. You tell the Rabbi to shake a leg 'cause I ain't got all friggin' day."

Colonel Micah considered the man a buffoon. Accordingly, he shifted his body away from him, trying to ignore him.

"No offense to you, bub, but what I'm carrying every Jew in Israel would eat hamhocks to learn."

Micah said nothing.

Fisher chattered on endlessly. About his trip to New Orleans, about some of his best friends being Jews, about how Steinberg would have to pay for the information he had and that he wasn't going to let the Rabbi—"no offense, mind you"—jew him down. He found his expression humorous and laughed until his gigantic belly bounced freely.

Fisher reached into his pants pocket, found a soiled handkerchief, blew his nose and wiped his teary eyes. Then he got up and walked to the bathroom. Micah heard a loud fart and the sound of his piss steaming into the bowl. "Aaaaaah," the corpulent investigator sighed. There was no sound of the toilet flushing, and the secretary grunted involuntarily in disgust when Fisher stepped out of the bathroom, wiping his hands on his trousers and zipping up his pants.

"Yeah," he said, finishing the chatter he'd kept up incessantly since his arrival. "You'd think I'd get some fuckin' respect around here. But do ya think I'm gettin' any fuckin' consideration?"

"Mr. Fisher! Please!" The secretary could stand no more.

"You please," yelled Fisher. Looking at Micah he said, "Here I am the onliest fuckin' guy who can finger a guy that knocked off that fuckin' Jew ambassador and they got me waitin' in the fuckin' lobby." Immediately, Pete knew

199

he'd said too much. Damn! He hadn't intended to run his fucking mouth like he had. But he had felt so good after his New Orleans success that he'd spent a little too much time at his favorite bar in midtown Manhattan. And whenever he got plastered, he said more than he ordinarily would say. And something told him that he'd said too much.

"What'd you say!" Colonel Micah leaped from his chair. The secretary, who'd tuned Pete out, had missed his comment about the ambassador.

"Nothin'," said Fisher. "I didn't say nothin'."

"Oh yes you did. Come with me." Micah seized the man's huge arm in a vise-like grip. "We have to talk."

"Hey! Wait a fuckin' minute," Fisher screamed. He tried to jerk his arm back. But Micah pressed a nerve beneath the private detective's armpit. Fisher had never experienced such pain before in his life.

"Alright already!" he hollered. "I'm comin' for Christ's sake."

Micah and Fisher hurried to the car which was parked near JDL headquarters. They both got into the backseat. Martin Kahn was at the wheel.

"Drive," Micah commanded a confused Kahn.

"Tell me everything you know," ordered Micah. For the first time Fisher noticed the man's foreign accent. He felt fear building up in his chest.

"What's in it for me?" asked the fat man.

Colonel Micah was tired and desperate. He had no patience now and his usual finesse suffered because of this. He pulled out a large pistol and buried it inside the folds in Fisher's fleshy belly.

"Quite possibly," he answered icily, "your life."

By the time they'd reached the Major Deegan expressway, Fisher had told them everything.

"And how do you get your reports to this Morgan?" asked

Micah, the gun still poking into Fisher's abdomen.

"I...I used to wait for him to call me. Now I send it to his post office box. In Chicago."

"Martin," barked Colonel Micah, "hand me that pack of photographs inside my briefcase." The case was on the seat next to Kahn. With one hand he opened the Samsonite and handed the envelope to Micah.

Micah handed the photographs to Fisher. "Are any of these men Bob Morgan?"

With hands shaking, Fisher looked at the pictures. They were of Anthony Vice, David Thomas and Eric Schofield.

"Yes. This one here. That's Morgan."

The picture was of Eric Schofield.

Later on, Martin Kahn looked at Colonel Micah with something akin to worship. "You were right. About everything!" the younger man gushed. "Pisces *is* on a new assignment and he *hasn't* left the country. And to think he's going to kill Elijah Muhammad. Wow!"

The Muslim leader was well known and widely detested in Israeli governmental circles.

Colonel Micah looked at Kahn with amusement. He was picking up American speech habits rapidly. He was also fulfilling his lifetime fantasy. He was an espionage agent, for real.

"But I still think we should have killed the fat man," said Martin. "He knows too much and he talks too much."

"You are forgetting that the secretary knows I left with him. She also has our names logged for appointments with Steinberg. We can't afford to have him turn up dead the very day we virtually kidnap him from the office. The potential conflagration would be immense," the Colonel explained pedantically.

"Yeah, but what if he blabs?" asked Kahn.

"We have already put the fear of God into the despicable

rodent. He'll not mouth a word. He knows we'll get him if he does.

Eric Schofield opened the post office box he'd rented in the name of Robert Morgan. He took out the large envelope sent to him by Fisher.

As he made his way through pedestrian traffic, he didn't see the young white man following several feet behind him.

When Schofield reached his car, the young man slid into the front seat of a car that was cruising in pace with him.

Colonel Abraham Micah and Agent Martin Kahn had found Pisces.

When Schofield reached his apartment it had already become dark. He got off the elevator and walked toward his place. To his surprise he found Gwendolyn Akbar outside his door, sitting on the floor. She was crying.

"Gwen! Gwen! What's the matter?"

"Oh Sean! Oh Sean!"

He opened the door and helped her into the apartment. He made her sit down. He got her a glass of spring water (she had said she didn't like spigot water). After allowing her to cry for several minutes, her body shaking with the force of her grief, he said, "Now tell me what's the matter, baby."

Her crying slowed a little. "He...he...oh, Sean." The crying began with renewed vigor. "He had a h-heart attack! The Messenger had a heart attack. He's in the hospital. Oh Sean, he might die. I heard the captain say he might die!" She was nearly hysterical.

Schofield squeezed her close, her body still shaking furiously with every sob. She was both grief stricken and filled with an unknown fear. What would life be like, how ever could she live, without the Messenger.

For many minutes Schofield just held her, letting her paint him with her tears.

When her sobs finally subsided, he carried her into his bedroom. He undressed her and put her to bed. She fell asleep more quickly than Eric had expected her to. The events of the day had exhausted her.

While Gwendolyn slept Schofield went over the plans in his mind. All of them were down the drain. He'd listened to the news. Elijah Muhammad had indeed suffered a massive heart attack and was in intensive care. Speculation was that he wouldn't survive.

Schofield struggled to keep cool. Calm down. A new plan. Get a new plan. Just wait and see what happens and devise a new plan accordingly.

When Gwen woke up, Eric had dinner already prepared. He wanted to serve her dinner in bed, but she wanted to get up. She walked into the kitchen in her panties and bra. Although her face was still lined with sorrow, Schofield had never seen anyone more beautiful.

In Boston, Isaac Payne—like the other Guardian Angels—had heard the news of Elijah's attack. He didn't know if the attack was somehow related to Schofield's mission or if this was a purely natural occurrence. He was starting to give up hope of stopping Schofield. Without help it was impossible at this late stage. Schofield had eluded him, almost as if he knew he was being pursued.

Schofield was a professional. He, Payne, was a lawyer unfamiliar with the techniques of international assassins. The last phone call had come from a phone booth less than a block away from Temple No. 2. Payne had gotten the feeling that Pisces had deliberately made his call so close to the Nation's headquarters to mock him. He had been totally outclassed. He knew now that he'd lost the battle. But the war was far from over. A new plan was forming in his mind.

Perhaps it was best that Farrakhan not gain the throne.

Undoubtedly, Farrakhan would soon tire of playing second fiddle to Wallace and would branch out on his own. Why not duplicate the work that'd been done in the Nation with the group that Farrakhan would inevitably form? Surely, with the experience he now had, he could accomplish the work in a few years as opposed to several decades. If he planned wisely he could even funnel some of the resources of the Guardian Angels into Farrakhan's movement.

No, he hadn't been beaten. A mere setback. For how long, he didn't know. But did not the Quran say that Allah is with those who patiently persevere? He would persevere. And he would win.

Martin Kahn's impatience had gotten the better of him again. "We should kill Pisces now!" he shouted at the Colonel. "It's clear that he's not going to hit Elijah now that the old bastard will probably die on his own."

But Abraham Micah was, if nothing else, a patient and methodical man when dealing with matters that required time to unfold. His gut instincts were that Elijah would recover. He'd done so many times before, to the chagrin of those who knew how dangerous he could potentially become.

The unique quality about Micah was his ability to perceive the larger issues and to peer into the future and to perceive what the future issues would be.

Elijah Muhammad would be a threat, in the future, to Israel; perhaps a bigger threat than the PLO. Not him individually, but his ideology. When the new class of educated Black Muslims cast aside their isolationism and seized a piece of the American political pie, they would be a force in foreign policy to be reckoned with. The mere chance that they could sway America's insurmountable power against Israel was something that had to be planned against.

Micah was looking twenty, thirty years into the future.

He well remembered how an obscure Austrian fanatic rose up from lance corporal to threaten the existence of every Jew on earth.

He would wait. If there was a single chance that Elijah Muhammad might recover, he wanted Pisces alive just long enough to complete his mission. Not a minute more.

Chapter Twenty-One

February, 1975

Colonel Abraham Micah's famed intuition had proven true once again. The Honorable Elijah Muhammad was recovering steadily. His health had improved to such an extent that the Messenger, over the protests of his family and top aides, was making arrangements to speak at the annual Saviour's Day convention.

Gwendolyn Akbar was one of the few secretaries who were allowed to visit the Messenger every day. She sat with him as long as she was permitted. These session permitted her a closeness to the Messenger that she hadn't previously enjoyed. She was one of those whom the Messenger had selected to read him his correspondence and to take dictation.

"When I am gone," he told her one afternoon, "read the Quran. If you want to talk to Allah, read the Quran. You will all forget me one day." When Gwen protested against that remark, he said, "Oh, yes, you will! You will forget Elijah and you'll curse me too. You'll curse the day I lifted you up from the mud. You will forget everything I have taught you just like Israel forgot what the Prophet Musa taught them. But my Saviour won't let me down. Allah will make you remember little Elijah. Allah will bring me back before your eyes. You will have to remember me again."

She was confused. "Dear Apostle, are you saying that you'll come back like they thought Jesus would? Was that part of scripture really talking about you?"

"Night and day for forty years I have preached and preached, but nobody understands. No, sister. I will not come back here in a physical body. And I won't be a spook either. But Almighty Allah, the Most Merciful, will bring about conditions that will force you to remember that what I taught you was the best."

"But Dear Apostle, that won't be for another several hundred years. You'll outlive Noah. I really believe that."

The Messenger of Allah's expression was sad and sympathetic. There was so much his poor followers didn't know. "Maybe, Sister, maybe Muhammad will live longer than Noah." He laughed a short little laugh that indicated that he was saying something with deeper meaning beneath the surface.

"When I'm gone, Sister Gwendolyn, you'll have the Quran. You'll have the Holy Quran. You'll have the Holy Quran and you'll have the signs of nature to guide you after me. And you will have a council of learned scientists who will study the scriptures and the wisdom the Saviour left me. And they will make the laws for the Nation of Islam."

"Dear Apostle, please don't speak like you're leaving us. Please."

"And a new Quran. Imagine that! Allah showed me in a vision. A new holy Quran. And he said I couldn't have it until I learned to read Arabic. It was in a new Arabic and the words were indented. They had depth. And the light shined up from the words on the page. And I was down in a valley by a stream and I was humming a song and I came upon the new Quran.''

"Is Allah going to reveal a new Quran to you, Dear Apostle?"

"Elijah lives in his people. I am the same as my people. As long as the Black Man lives, Elijah lives."

The Messenger then changed the subject. "You've changed, Sister Gwendolyn. Allah has let me see that you have changed." He paused. Then he said, "Marry him, Sister. Maybe God will bless you to have a whole lot of little children."

"Yes, sir, Dear Apostle."

Then he started coughing, the pain racking his frail body. The doctor came in and told Gwendolyn to leave. The Messenger was still very weak and needed lots of rest.

Each evening Gwen recounted her experiences at the hospital. Eric had gotten her to describe the building in detail and her descriptions were so thorough that he felt he knew the building as well as its architect.

A plan had formed in Schofield's mind. He wrote, in Arabic, the details of his plan on a notepad. Should Gwen stumble across his plans she couldn't read them, though he didn't think she would invade his privacy, because she wasn't able to read Arabic.

Some of the particulars he had yet to iron out, but he wrote down one possibility. There was another that he had in his mind. He decided to keep it there instead of committing it to paper until he tested the feasibility of his first idea. One thing at a time.

The next morning he was at the chemistry department of the University of Chicago. He had found that people, especially men, speak more freely with an unknown woman than with an unknown man. Consequently, Schofield had disguised himself as a woman and he spoke with an enraptured chemist for hours.

After a promise of a dinner date the chemist provided "Donna Barker," whom he thought was a zoologist, with a vial of digitalis, a heart stimulant which could, with sufficient dosage, produce a heart attack. A large dose, he warned the zoologist, would not only kill an animal, it would kill a human.

After leaving the lovestruck chemist, Eric Schofield decided it was time he got a first-hand look at Mercy Douglas Hospital.

The tall, attractive "woman" moved freely through the hospital corridors. Ironically, Gwendolyn Akbar, on her way to visit Elijah saw the "woman" and smiled a greeting to her.

Eric Schofield smiled back.

"You got a phone call, Mister Fisher," chimed Maria Perez.

"Fuck the call!" Pete Fisher flung his cup of cold coffee at the startled Puerto Rican.

Fuck her! Fuck them all! Everybody pissed on Pete Fisher. All of them. The fucking Army! The fucking law school! His fucking wife had left him. The police hated his guts. Now the fuckin' Jews were pissin' in his face. Shit! He was sick of it. Sick and tired of it.

Pushed around by crummy Jews! And they threatened to kill him! Shit! He was already dead. He was already in the fucking casket. They just forgot to push the dirt on top of him. If a man couldn't do his thing, shit! He was as good as dead!

No, he'd taken too much. He wouldn't be pushed around again. Never again. This time he was going to do the pushing.

209

"Maria," he called sweetly. "Maria, I'm sorry. Come here, baby. I'm sorry."

The girl smiled, sniffling, came hesitantly into the office. Coffee stains were on her skirt and blouse.

Fisher pulled out his wallet and offered her fifty dollars. "Here, hon. Buy yourself a dress or somethin'."

Maria was astonished. She'd never known Pete Fisher to be anything except an asshole and a slob.

But Fisher thought that this new generosity was appropriate. A man should be nice to others, Fisher believed, when he was going away to die.

Colonel Micah and Kahn had made certain that Schofield was spending the night with Gwendolyn before they burglarized his apartment. It was Kahn who found the notebook. He couldn't understand Arabic writing, but Micah could.

Micah read it and saw a masterful plan. The man, Micah admitted, was a genius. And the old war horse felt a strange kinship with the black American killer.

Schofield would kill Elijah when the FOI security around him was at its weakest during the Saviour's Day preparations. He would disguise himself as a nurse and administer the drug to Elijah. He would lock the door upon departure, telling the bodyguards to allow Muhammad to sleep.

A simple but brilliant plan.

All they had to do was wait for the phoney nurse to come out of the hospital and eliminate him. At that point they would have killed the proverbial two birds with one stone: Pisces *and* Elijah Muhammad.

The next morning when Schofield returned to his apartment he had a vague feeling that something was wrong. He checked his apartment and found nothing out of place. Yet he could feel that something was not quite right. He shrugged off the feeling and left to check his mailbox.

Instead of finding mail at his box, the surprised assassin found Pete Fisher.

Fisher was looking from left to right, his eyes wide with terror.

"Morgan! Morgan, we gotta talk. There's no time!"

"Fisher! What are you doing here?"

"No time. They may be here. We gotta talk, now!"

The fat man pulled Schofield by the arm until they reached his rental car. Fisher shot out of the parking space and sped away. For many minutes he glanced repeatedly into the rearview mirror to see if he was being followed.

"The Israelis are after ya," he said at length. "They made me tell 'em everything. They know that you're really Schofield and that you killed that ambassador. They were gonna kill me too—I could feel it—but they changed their minds."

Schofield looked at the corpulent man whose face was white with fear. Anger rushed into Schofield's own face but he forced himself to calm down, made the blood that had rushed to his head subside.

"Tell me everything you told them. Don't leave out a single word."

When Fisher had finished, Eric, losing control, banged his fist against the dashboard. "God damn!" he yelled.

Get control of yourself. A plan. That's all you need. That's all that's ever needed. Planning. A new plan. Must always be in control.

"Pull in here," Schofield commanded after seeing a liquor store. "Stop here a moment."

Schofield got out and went into the liquor store. When he came back he was carrying a bottle of whiskey in a brown paper bag.

"Drink," Schofield ordered Fisher after he got into the

car.

"Why?" said a frightened Pete Fisher.

"Because I'm going to kill those two Israelis. And I want you in the police drunk tank when it happens. That way you won't possibly be a suspect."

Fisher smiled. "That's pretty smart." Damn, this guy Morgan wasn't so bad. Nobody had ever worried about his well-being before.

Several minutes later Fisher vomited.

"Drink," commanded Schofield.

"I can't handle no more, man. Honest."

"Drink, I said!"

Fisher gulped down some more whiskey, spit most of it back up, farted and passed out. They were parked on a secluded Westside street.

Schofield pushed the heavy man onto the passenger seat and got behind the wheel. He drove to the Northside of Chicago onto North Avenue. He drove the car several blocks up North Avenue. Then he turned the vehicle around and drove down. North Avenue is a steep hill. It's a favorite spot for bicycle joyriders and children on sleds during the winter.

Schofield turned off the motor and allowed the car to coast downhill. It coasted faster and faster. It approached the intersection at North Wells Street. Three automobiles slammed into the unmanned vehicle, twisting and crushing it.

Peter Fisher, unconscious and drunk, never knew what had taken away his life. Before the ambulance arrived, Fisher was dead.

Eric Schofield heard the crunch of metal and the screams of the people nearby. He walked on for several miles before hailing a cab that took him to his car that was still parked near the post office.

He saw something attached to his windshield. He examined it. He'd been given a parking ticket.

Chapter Twenty-Two

February 25, 1975
1:15 A.M.

The muscles in Schofield's face were tight and his expression was grim when he drove away from the hotel where he'd left the prostitute Melody. Everything depended upon her and how much she wanted the grant he'd offered her. She was his insurance. If she failed to come through there'd be a bloody mess in front of Mercy Douglas Hospital. Some of it would likely be his.

According to the dead private detective, one of the Israelis hunting him had been referred to as "Colonel Micah." That could be none other than the legendary Colonel Abraham Micah, mastermind behind many of the renowned tactics of MOSSAD.

Schofield would prefer facing an army of Vietcong. He had studied Micah years ago when he was in Africa. The long arm of MOSSAD reached every continent and was especially active on the black continent. He had kept abreast of Mica's activities because he never knew when he might have to confront the feared Israeli. As Schofield worked both sides of the political fence, he didn't know if his first meeting with Micah would be as enemy or ally. But he had wanted to be prepared.

Now he knew that it would be as enemies that they would encounter each other.

Micah had been widely touted as the next director of MOSSAD. When he had resigned in anger, Schofield had breathed a sigh of relief. He foolishly thought that he would be able to avoid an eventual confrontation with the man. Several Arabs were interested in eliminating Israeli political figures and Schofield didn't want Micah after him.

Now he realized that it was inevitable that they would meet. And it was equally inevitable that only one of them would survive the encounter.

But first, there was work to do. Schofield was glad he hadn't committed his auxiliary plan to paper. He wondered, with a smile, if he was psychic.

Alliance Window Washers and Janitorial Services was the largest business of its kind in Chicago. When the company offices were broken into and nothing was taken, police were flummoxed.

Inside the offices were typewriters, calculators, Xerox machines and several thousand dollars. But the burglar had declined to remove any of it. He had taken, as far as they could tell, nothing.

The police did determine that several desks had been pried open. The burglar was evidently searching for something specific. No one had the slightest idea what it was.

Eric Schofield was playing his last ace. He had learned that Alliance was contracted to clean Mercy Douglas

Hospital's windows by telephoning the hospital's administrator and pretending to be a self-employed window washer looking to add Mercy Douglas to his clientele.

The administrator had said, "It's highly improbable that we could utilize your expertise. You see, we're under contract with Alliance."

"Well, thanks anyway," said Schofield. He hung up and reached for the Yellow Pages. He let his fingers do some walking and he found Alliance's address. Schofield knew what to do then. He needed to know what dates they were scheduled to clean the windows of Mercy Douglas and who the employee was who did the work.

It was Schofield who burglarized Alliance's offices. He had photocopied pages from their route book and their contractual arrangements.

He'd found what he was seeking.

Bernie Clay lived alone above the Dew Drop Inn, a speakeasy on Halstead Avenue. He had grown accustomed to the pounding music, the loud laughter, the incessant speech. The floor of his efficiency vibrated with the rhythm of James Brown's "The Big Payback." But none of this affected Bernie's sleep. He slept soundly and, in fact, had been sleeping for hours. He had to get up early that morning to wash the windows at Mercy Douglas Hospital. He went to bed early because he intended to get an early start.

The van he drove bearing Alliance's logo of two clasped hands was parked across the street.

Owing to the pulsating music and his slumber, Bernie couldn't possibly hear the lock on his door being picked. When Eric Schofield crept into the apartment and walked over to Clay's bed, he saw a smile on the sleeping man's face.

Schofield studied the ice pick he held in his hand. He knelt down beside the bed and gently placed the point of the pick

215

behind Bernie's left ear. He thrust the ice pick past the soft flesh beneath the skull and up into the unsuspecting man's head. In seconds, Bernie was dead.

Schofield spent a few minutes picking up Clay's Alliance uniform and the keys to the van.

Chapter Twenty-Three

February 25, 1975
7:30 A.M.

Eric Schofield, clad in an Alliance uniform, presented himself at the main desk of Mercy Douglas Hospital. He told the receptionist that he was there to do the windows.

"Where's Bernie?" the woman asked, concerned.

"Down with the flu. I had to fill in for him today. On my day off, no less."

"Take the freight elevator," she said looking at Schofield's equipment. "It's over to the left. You can ride it up to the roof." Schofield turned and headed for the elevator. "Give Bernie my regards," she hollered after Schofield.

When Melody, dressed smartly in nurse's white, approached Mercy Douglas Hospital, Martin Kahn, seated in a blue Oldsmobile, spoke into a walkie-talkie.

"Pisces," he said, "has arrived. He's disguised as a nurse.

The disguise looks so authentic that it's hard to tell he's not a woman.''

But the Israeli knew it was Schofield because they had obtained photographs of every female employee at the hospital, and this one was not one of them. Therefore, this imposter had to be Pisces.

Kahn's voice, metallic and mechanical in sound, reached Colonel Micah who had been circling the hospital on foot.

"Are you sure it's Pisces?" asked the Colonel.

"Yes! Yes, I'm sure. Same height, same basic build. Same complexion. It's him. No female employees are even close to six feet tall.''

Colonel Micah hurried to join the young agent in the Oldsmobile. They set up and awaited Schofield's exit.

No one noticed the man on the roof who was dropping down, supported by ropes, to wash the hospital's windows.

There were FOI members posted outside of Elijah Muhammad's hospital room twenty-four hours a day. There were also Fruit soldiers who occasionally patrolled the corridors and checked storage places for anything that might resemble a bomb. They knew that there were forces in this country and beyond who wanted Muhammad out of the way so badly that they would think nothing of blowing up the whole hospital just to get him.

For all the security arrangements that had been instituted— and which had weakened due to the lengthy duration of Muhammad's stay—Eric Schofield was amused to find that the window of Elijah's room was not locked.

Elijah Muhammad was resting comfortably. He remained asleep as Schofield raised the window slowly and quietly. The assassin stood perched on the window sill and gazed at the aged Muslim leader. Schofield unhooked the straps which supported him and stepped into the room.

218

He looked at this man who had led the Nation of Islam for four decades and a strange sadness came over his heart. Schofield was anything but a religious man and he regarded Elijah's claim on the messengership of God to be so much crap. Yet this man had accomplished what no other leader had been able to do among blacks. He had instilled dignity and purpose into this followers and he was an inspiration to non-Muslims as well.

The Honorable Elijah Muhammad had taken the needle out of thousands of black junkies' arms. His teachings had revirginated countless prostitutes and reformed thousands of criminals.

Schofield, for some reason, remembered something that James Baldwin had written about Muhammad in his book, *The Fire Next Time.* It was a statement of which the Muslims were especially proud. It even appeared on the jacket of Elijah's *Message to the Black Man in America.* Baldwin had written that ''Elijah Muhammad has been able to do what generations of welfare workers and committees and resolutions and reports and housing projects and playgrounds have failed to do. He has done all these things, which our Christian church has spectacularly failed to do.''

Schofield thought of the Muslim enterprises that had sprung up in every city from coast to coast. They were, by and large, humble establishments when measured against corporate America. But they were growing and had been founded in the true American tradition.

The man sleeping before him was the power behind the new strength that he witnessed now blooming within the national black community. This strength was reflected especially in the young. The inferiority complexes were disappearing. So was the hesitance that seemed to grip blacks whenever they were around whites. And the terror of the white race that he had seen in blacks was all but eradicated. The man who lay before him was responsible for much of the transformation.

Would all this progress end with the thrust of the needle filled with digitalis into Elijah's arm? Would the construction end with the death of the architect?

Or would the followers embrace the principles as they had once embraced the man? And what of Elijah's successor? Who would that man be? Could he continue the work of the leader? Could anyone?

Schofield was sure that the old men who had hired him to murder Elijah Muhammad had someone in mind to replace Muhammad. But who would that person be?

Such concerns, Schofield decided, were not for him to worry about. He had been paid to do a job and he either would or he wouldn't.

He looked at his watch. It was 8:05 A.M. One more step and his job was finished.

Elijah Muhammad's face bore the appearance of serenity and assurance. Schofield briefly considered the thought that maybe angels were, that moment, telling him that it was all right; that his work would be fulfilled. But Schofield dismissed that thought as ludicrous. He didn't believe in such things.

He gently pulled back the covers and lifted the Messenger's frail arm. He lay the arm, palm up, on the bed.

Schofield took out the hypodermic needle containing the digitalis. He knew that the drug would turn up in an autopsy. But he doubted if hospital officials would order one for the old man. And the police wouldn't either, unless foul play was suspected.

Schofield removed the cap from the needle. He poked the vein inside of Elijah's elbow. Then he stuck the needle deeply into the vein. He pushed down on the plunger allowing the

220

deadly fluid to flow into the Messenger's blood stream.

Elijah's eyes shot open. He clutched at his chest, knocking the needle to the tiled floor in the movement. He tried to call out, to scream, but he only succeeded in gasping and choking.

His chest heaved and his face twisted in agony. Muhammad raised his upper body into a sitting position briefly and then was slammed back against the mattress by a massive muscle contraction. His eyes rolled up into his head and Schofield saw the whites through the open eyelids.

Elijah Muhammad was dead.

Chapter Twenty-Four

At exactly 8:10 A.M., Melody got to her feet in the Mercy Douglas Hospital cafeteria. She walked swiftly to the hospital's exit. She reached the sidewalk, paused for a moment, then walked quickly to her left.

She heard a man's voice yelling, "Stop! Pisces, stop!" She thought it was the man who wanted to play the weird chase game. She wondered briefly how she would spend her thousand dollars. Then she ran.

Colonel Abraham Micah didn't chase her. Instead, he fired twice at her fleeing form. Both bullets tore into her. One in the back, the other in the head.

She died before she hit the pavement. Her face—what remained of it—floated in a puddle of blood that had risen up around her head.

"You got him! You actually got him!" screamed a gleeful Martin Kahn when Micah returned to the car.

"You did it!" yelled Kahn, incredulous. "You killed Pisces!"

"Get away from here. Fast!"

Chapter Twenty-Five

Colonel Abraham Micah and Martin Kahn returned to New York and remained there for several days. They both agreed that a short sabbatical was in order after the gruelling experience of tracking and killing Pisces.

Martin, especially, was eager to sample New York's famed nightlife.

But the period of rest had ended—all too quickly—and they were ready to return to Israel. They were packed and prepared to drive to Kennedy Airport where they would board their flight to the Mideast.

Martin's mood, since the Pisces affair, had been euphoric. Nobody, he felt, would be able to keep him out of the action now. He had gotten real field experience and had worked under the instruction and command of an acknowledged master. He felt like a million bucks.

Colonel Micah's mood wasn't nearly as euphoric as was

Kahn's. Something that he couldn't quite put a finger on was bothering him. There had been something in the killing of Pisces that hadn't been in his direct control. There was something that troubled him. Yet he couldn't remember what it was, but his instinct told him that something was wrong.

The Colonel approached the passenger side of the rented Pontiac. Kahn was going to drive. He stuck the key into the door to unlock it.

The afternoon sun struck Micah directly in the eyes. He was partially blinded by the rays of the sun.

While Kahn was twisting the key, Micah remembered what was bothering him about the whole affair. It had been Kahn who had identified the nurse as Schofield, and Kahn's experience was nil.

He looked at Martin, a confused expression on his face. Martin was opening the door.

"Noooo!" screamed Micah.

The cry came too late. The automobile exploded, ripping the two men's bodies to shreds.

The illustrious career of Colonel Abraham Micah had come to an end. And Martin Kahn's brief appearance on the theatre of international intrigue had been terminated.

Eric Schofield had killed them both.

Epilogue

The funeral procession rolled into Lincoln Greatest Memorial Cemetery. The body of Rochelle Kennedy aka Melody was carried by pallbearers to the unmarked grave.

The preacher, Rev. Dwayne Atkinson, preached about the ways of the Lord cleansing the harm that the ways of the world had done to the innocent soul about to be put to rest.

Mrs. Agatha Kennedy sobbed helplessly at the sight of the casket bearing her daughter's body being lowered inside the hollow earth.

She hardly noticed the slim, well-dressed man step up beside her. The man placed his arm around her tenderly.

"Mrs. Kennedy, I'm very sorry about what happened," the man said. The woman simply nodded. She wanted to be alone with her grief.

"Here, this belonged to her," the man said, pressing an envelope into the woman's hand.

She opened it, not being concerned about etiquette. She found ten one-hundred dollar bills.

"What's this?" she said to the man, tears still running from her eyes.

"Some money. It was hers. I know she would want you to have it."

"Who are you?"

"A friend."

"Was you...was you her *pimp?* If you are that dirty bastard, then I don't want your blood money, you hear?"

"Yes, ma'am. But I'm not a pimp. Just a friend of hers."

The woman pushed the money down into her bra.

"I'm really sorry, ma'am," the man said. Then he walked away and opened the door of a Mercedes sportscar.

Melody's little brother, Henry, was curious about the man who'd been talking to his mother. Henry followed him at a safe distance to his car.

What struck the boy's eye was a key chain that the man took out of his pocket. It looked like real gold. And on the medallion were two fish. The astrological sign.

Pisces.

TO KILL A BLACK MAN

By Louis E. Lomax

A compelling dual biography of the two men who changed America's way of thinking—Malcolm X and Martin Luther King, Jr.

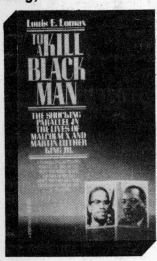

Louis E. Lomax was a close friend to both Malcolm X and Dr. Martin Luther King, Jr. In this dual biography, he includes much that Malcolm X did not tell in his autobiography and dissects Malcolm's famous letters. Lomax writes with the sympathy and understanding of a friend but he is also quick to point out the shortcomings of both Dr. King and Malcolm X—and what he believed was the reasons for their failure to achieve their goals and to obtain the full support of all their people. And he does not hesitate in pointing a finger at those he believes to be responsible for the deaths of his friends. "A valuable addition to the available information on the murders of Martin Luther King, Jr. and Malcolm X," says the *Litterair Passport*. Louis Lomax gained national prominence with such books as *The Black Revolt, When The Word Is Given*, and *To Kill A Black Man*. At the time of his death in an automobile accident he was a professor at Hofstra University.

JESSE JACKSON

By Eddie Stone

An Intimate Portrait of the Most Charismatic Man in American Politics

He's dynamic, charming, intelligent and has more charisma than any man to rocket into the American political arena since John F. Kennedy. One of the country's most popular black leaders, he is not without his critics. To many he is just too flamboyant, others find his political ideas somewhat vague, still others call him a blatant opportunist. Nevertheless he has proven he can pull in the votes whether it's in Vermont, or Mississippi, or Michigan. Jackson will play a major—and far reaching—role in American politics in the years to come.

DOGHOUSE

BY JIM DAWSON

When a desperate young singer off the streets gives private eye Maceo "Doghouse" Washington her last two crumpled twenty dollar bills to find her boyfriend, he finds himself up against more than he can handle. A sleazy record producer demands that he surrender his client, a switchblade-toting doo-wop group is trying to kill him, two corrupt vice cops are dogging him, and a 250-pound ex-blues queen just wants him out of the way. To make matters worse, his client disappears and if he can't find her, his life is worth less than the forty dollars she gave him.

TRACKING MODE

BY JOHN SPRINGS III

Rupert Stone mourns the loss of his family, victims of a government cover-up to protect a witness against the Mafia. There was only one thing Stone could do to get his life back together—find the man responsible and eliminate him. An officer of the law himself, Stone knows what needs to be done to accomplish his mission, and relies on the tricks of his trade to uncover the truth and mete out justice to those who deserve it. Double-cross, rage and death are left in Stone's wake as he sets his mind in...Tracking Mode.

JOHN SPRINGS III
The bestselling author of KANSAS

A chilling, relentless pursuit of justice.

BLACK BAIT

BY LEO GUILD

She's passionate, bold, and goes after what she wants. And what she wants is you! Or, to put that another way, your money. Sure, she's got a dazzling smile; and she's a master of kinky sex. But underneath that kittenish exterior is a petulant and mercurial woman—a woman who always gets what she wants. One way or the other... Leo Guild, author of the best-selling *The Girl Who Loved Black*, tells the true and shocking story of a gambling woman with a heart of gold, nerves of steel and backbone of ice. You'll never forget Lila!

JACK JOHNSON

BY ROBERT H. DECOY

The life of Jack Johnson, the first Afro-American Heavyweight Champion of the world, is the story of Civil Rights in the first half of the twentieth century.

Single-handedly, he stood up against the boxing kingpins, the KKK, and the United States Government. He was the man whom William Jennings Bryan called "a nigger" and the World Heavyweight Champion that Winston Churchill said was not welcome in England. Booker T. Washington condemned him for "rocking the boat" and Jack London, then America's favorite writer, sent out a call for The Great White Hope—a white boxer who could defeat him and "uphold the honor of white people."

Robert deCoy, author of the controversial best-seller, *The Nigger Bible,* knew Johnson well, and, therefore was able to set the record straight. This is the life of Jack Johnson as it really happened.

0-87067-581-8 $4.95

JACK JOHNSON
THE BIG BLACK FIRE
By Robert H. deCoy

UNCENSORED BIOGRAPHY OF
THE FIRST BLACK HEAVYWEIGHT CHAMPION

SUNDAY HELL

BY BUTCH HOLMES

Rocket Hunter is the most gifted black quarterback ever to play college football. He can make a pigskin talk pig latin! And his burning ambition is to be the first black superstar quarterback in pro football—the Sunday game—and make a few million dollars. Two obstacles stand in his way: Lena, a sweet sixteen sexpot who is determined to bed down with Rocket—even if the act breaks the rules and the law; and Leda, a voluptuous white chick who is convinced that love is more important than any ambition. Sunday Hell is a hard, gritty journey into the world of the black superjock and the success-crazy men and women who manipulate big time athletics.

THE ROOTWORKER

BY GLENDA DUMAS

Sissie was in love for the very first time, deeply and completely. Dano was everything she'd ever dreamed of and more. But he was an outsider...and outsiders were looked on with something worse than suspicion in the small North Carolina town where Sissie grew up. Her parents begged her not to bring him there, not to bring him home with her. But she felt it was important. Her parents were good people and had raised her to be. They couldn't hurt anyone she loved. But Sissie was wrong. They were waiting and watching and they destroyed for the pure pleasure of it! They were members of a Satanic cult, a cult devoted to evil, the cult of the Rootworkers.

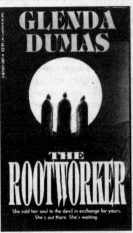

GLENDA DUMAS

THE ROOTWORKER

She sold her soul to the devil in exchange for yours. She's out there. She's waiting.

A GARDEN OF BITTER HERBS

BY ROXANN LARRISON

Separated as toddlers, Rosemary and Sage lived lives filled with degradation and oppression during the height of the slave plantation era. Rosemary, determined to rid herself of her master who treated her no better than a farm animal—except when he wanted his pleasure—would stop at nothing to gain her freedom. Sage, although not treated as badly as his sister, nonetheless woke to each day with the heavy chain of slavery wrapped tightly around his soul. After reuniting, Rosemary and Sage make plans to escape the pain and humiliation together. The stakes are either freedom . . . or death

The stakes are freedom...or death!

A GARDEN OF BITTER HERBS

Roxann Larrison

MELROSE SQUARE
BLACK AMERICAN
SERIES

These highly acclaimed quality format paperback
editions are profusely illustrated, meticulously
researched and fully indexed. $3.95 ea.

☐ **NAT TURNER:** Prophet and Slave Revolt Leader

☐ **PAUL ROBESON:** Athlete, Actor, Singer, Activist

☐ **ELLA FITZGERALD:** First Lady of American Song

☐ **MALCOLM X:** Militant Black Leader

☐ **JACKIE ROBINSON:** First Black in Professional Baseball

☐ **MATTHEW HENSON:** Arctic Explorer

☐ **SCOTT JOPLIN:** Composer

☐ **LOUIS ARMSTRONG:** Musician

☐ **SOJOURNER TRUTH:** Antislavery Activist

☐ **CHESTER HIMES:** Author and Civil Rights Pioneer

☐ **BILLIE HOLIDAY:** Singer

☐ **RICHARD WRIGHT:** Author

☐ **ALTHEA GIBSON:** Tennis Champion

☐ **JAMES BALDWIN:** Author

☐ **WILMA RUDOLPH:** Champion Athlete

☐ **SIDNEY POITIER:** Actor

☐ **JESSE OWENS:** Olympic Superstar

☐ **MARCUS GARVEY:** Black Nationalist Leader

☐ **JOE LOUIS:** Boxing Champion

☐ **HARRY BELAFONTE:** Singer & Actor

☐ **LENA HORNE:** Singer & Actor

BUFFALO SOLDIER

BY CHARLES R. GOODMAN

Luke joined the cavalry because working with horses was all he'd ever done and it was a job he loved. However, he soon found himself in Texas fighting Indians under the command of an officer whose only pleasure in life was killing. The carnage sickened Luke to the point that during an attack on a small camp, occupied only by women, children and the aged, he shot his commanding officer and became a fugitive. As a result of the kind-

ness he'd shown a wounded old man from the camp, he was adopted by the Commanche. Upon proving himself, he was promoted to war chief—and led the attacks on the "Buffalo Soldiers," as the black cavalry-men were called by the Indians. Once Luke began to think of himself as a Commanche, he saw the unfairness of it all. All the Indians wanted was to be left alone. But that was not to be. Charles Goodman has written the tragic epic of the savage and near complete extermination of the Native American as seen through the eyes of a Buffalo Soldier.